A Choice of Heaven

J. M. SCOTT

A Choice of Heaven

E. P. DUTTON & CO., INC.
New York   1960

Library of Congress Catalog Card Number: 60-5976

A Choice of Heaven

Chapter One

I

At a quarter past ten Mr. Pinkerton arrived at the office. His secretary followed him into his room and a few minutes later came out again. He was closing the door when the Old Man said to him, "Send in Mr. Skinner."

"I am sorry, sir, Mr. Skinner has not come to the office today," the secretary said.

"Why? What's happened?"

"I can't say, sir. I suppose he must be ill."

"Skinner ill!"

The secretary remained waiting attentively until at last his employer dropped his eyes and began studying his mail. Then he softly closed the door.

Most of the clerks overheard this conversation and wondered at the Old Man's restraint. They were afraid that it might prove the calm before a storm.

Although the office of Pinkerton and Powell was not imposing—it was in a narrow street called Angel's Way at the eastern end of the City—it was the most important of its particular line, one of those business houses which have contributed to the romance of London River. For the firm reached out through correspondence and cargo vessels to some of the farthest and most colourful corners of

I

the world. It dealt in shagreen, pearls, mother-of-pearl shell, copra—the treasures of the Orient and tropical seas. There were buying centres and development centres run by local, English-speaking agents scattered over the thousands of miles between Arabia and the American side of the Pacific. As far as the clerks were concerned it was a business like any other—except that it was so complicated. Mr. Skinner, the chief clerk, had been in the firm longer than the Old Man. He had been taken on as a lad of fifteen by Mr. Pinkerton's father. He had everything at his finger-tips. Everybody, from the humblest member to the junior partner—to the Old Man himself—had come to depend upon the chief clerk's modestly-given information and advice. Nobody had ever known him to be absent before. They had taken him for granted. Now they missed him.

The day worked out as badly as they had feared it might. No one seemed to know the answer to any question. Everyone kicked the man below him, and the office boy kicked the cat. They were glad to go home.

My grandfather remained behind that evening. It was he who told me most of this story. I remember him as a fine old patriarch who collected characters and loved to talk about them at great length. We always called him G.P., which stood for grand-parent and happened to be his initials as well. He was distantly related to Mr. Pinkerton and he had then recently joined the firm as a gentleman-apprentice. He was supposed to be learning the ropes. But he was not that evening working at the firm's business. He had the collector's passion and he was just then engaged in making a collection of London insects. He had secured several specimens during the day

2

and he wanted to kill them, set them in suitable lifelike attitudes and then paint their portraits. For this delicate and imaginative work he preferred the peace of the empty office to the exacting and critical atmosphere of his home, with numerous brothers and sisters.

Shut into his little box-like room, G.P. was absorbed in this work when he became vaguely conscious of sounds where there should have been silence.

He sat back in his chair, listening and wondering. He could no longer hear anything, but he was disturbed. At last he got up and went out into the side passage, then round the corner of the main corridor. For comfort he had exchanged his boots for carpet slippers so he made no noise.

The door of Mr. Pinkerton's secretary's room was ajar and a light shone through the opening. This light was faint and might have come from the inner room. If the Old Man had returned it could do no harm for a young apprentice to show himself—still apparently hard at work yet alert for the safety of the office. G.P. went into the secretary's room.

In the doorway he stopped, holding his breath. The safe was wide open. In front of it, with his back to G.P., stood a man, one hand holding a lantern above his head while his other hand searched among the contents of the safe.

G.P. was not consciously afraid. But he was utterly taken by surprise. He was frozen. He did nothing.

The other finished what he was engaged upon, closed the safe door and lowered the lantern to turn the key in the lock. This action threw the upper part of his body into clear silhouette. G.P. recognised the chief clerk.

3

He breathed out like a sigh of relief, "Hello, Mr. Skinner."

Skinner was a man of between forty and fifty, on the small side but well made, alert in manner. He had a way of looking at one over the top of his spectacles with a kindly, quizzical expression. G.P. and he were particular friends—with something of the sergeant-major to junior subaltern relationship. The chief clerk had helped him a lot in finding his feet in the organisation, by saving him from errors and by coaching him up for the tour of the buying and development centres which he had been promised if he proved his mettle.

Now Skinner turned, and G.P. was shocked because he scarcely recognised his face. It had an other-world look, and—it might have been the lantern—the eyes seemed to glow with a rich and brilliant light.

"Oh, it's you, Mr. Partridge," said the chief clerk after a perceptible pause, and smiled.

"Yes," said G.P. "I am glad to see you are not ill. We thought——"

"Yes . . . You are working late."

"I had something to do."

"That's right. You'll get on, sir. You'll get your chance. Listen——" Skinner checked himself. When he spoke again it was in his ordinary office voice. "I wonder, sir, if you would be so kind as to do something for me— give this key to Mr. Pinkerton in the morning. Thank you, sir. Thank you for—for your friendship."

Skinner suddenly shook hands, and then was gone.

G.P.'s first instinct was to follow and ask questions. But instead he went back to his room and in the light looked at the large key he had been given. He recognised it as that of the office door. That, surely, could only mean that Skinner did not mean to return to the office. But he had kept the key of the safe.

The fingers of G.P. began again their delicate task of spreading out the wings of the dead insects so that when rigor mortis should set in they would be displayed to the best advantage. But his mind was not entirely on his hobby. He immediately dismissed the thought that Skinner might have had any dishonest intention. The confidant of the partners, the holder of the safe key, was above suspicion. Apart from that, Skinner was—Skinner. All the same, he had behaved strangely. And he had looked so strange, so excited.

Next morning Skinner failed to appear at the office. G.P. waited for Mr. Pinkerton's arrival, and as soon as possible went to see him.

Mr. Pinkerton was a large man with a high colour which suggested good living and bad temper.

"What the devil are you doing with that?" he asked, referring to the key which G.P. held in his hand.

G.P. described the incident of the night before.

The Old Man pondered for a little while, rubbing his face so hard that the features were squashed out of place. Then he said, "My compliments to Mr. Powell, and ask him if he can spare me a few minutes. Come back yourself."

Mr. Powell was the physical antithesis of Mr. Pinkerton —small, lean, sharp-featured. He had been in other businesses before buying his present partnership some ten years previously.

G.P. repeated his story before the two partners, after which Mr. Powell cross-examined him.

5

"Did Skinner take anything out of the safe?"

"I think he took a bag."

"Did you ask him why he acted as he did?"

"No, sir. I supposed he was engaged in some auditing work at home."

"Did he look ill?"

"No, sir. In fact he seemed in particularly good spirits—although he subdued them, of course."

"Of course," said Mr. Pinkerton, and unexpectedly laughed. His partner glanced at him and he added, "Skinner is the soul of restraint. I trained him myself."

"The first thing to do is to check the contents of the safe," said Mr. Powell.

"Very well," Mr. Pinkerton agreed. "We will do it as a matter of form. But I can tell you now that we will find everything in order. Skinner lives for the good of this firm. He kept the key to the safe because he could only give that to me personally."

In a curtained annexe to the senior partner's room was a large table on which maps and papers were sometimes spread. Now the contents of the safe were arranged upon it and a comparison started with the book entries. The firm's books, in Skinner's hand, were as clear as account books can be. Yet the task of checking was slow, for not only was money involved but also bags of pearls, valuable samples of different sorts.

While G.P. was busily engaged on this complicated work the secretary announced that a lady had called to see Mr. Pinkerton.

"I told you that I was not to be disturbed," the senior partner said angrily.

"It is Mrs. Skinner—Mr. Skinner's wife," the secretary

answered, and perhaps enjoyed the moment of triumph which he thus achieved.

When the lady was shown in, G.P. from his semi-concealed position looked at her with interest. Friendly though he had been with Skinner, he had not known of her existence. As far as he was aware, the chief clerk had never spoken to any of his colleagues about his private life. G.P. sympathised. If he had been married to Mrs. Skinner he would have kept quiet about it.

She held a handkerchief to her eyes and sniffed as she talked. She had come for news of her husband who, she said, had disappeared. Mr. Pinkerton replied sympathetically that he had no news but that if Mrs. Skinner would tell him everything that had happened they would no doubt find her husband very soon.

Mrs. Skinner had little to tell. She had last seen Skinner the morning before. It had been a morning like any other during the twenty-three years of their married life. He had brought her tea in bed. She had cooked his breakfast. He had eaten it behind his newspaper—"the foreign one he always got for the office". Mr. Pinkerton raised his eyebrows. But he did not interrupt Mrs. Skinner to question her about a newspaper.

She had addressed a remark to Skinner, she said. He did not answer. She spoke again. Still he did not answer —not even grunt. Although, as she admitted, she ought to have been used to such treatment by that time, she felt a hot flood of indignation. Why should she not be entertained as other women were? She asked him this. He did not answer. Exasperated beyond all control, she snatched the newspaper away.

Skinner, a piece of bread and marmalade held in midair, was staring in front of him. He blinked. Then—still without speaking—he rose and reached for the newspaper.

Mrs. Skinner put it behind her back.

Ordinarily this would have been quite enough. But he persisted. He actually laid hands upon her. Although he did not look it, he was as strong as anything. He quite hurt her while recovering his wretched, unintelligible newspaper. Then he went out of the room.

She waited for him to come back and apologise. He did not come. At last she went to look for him, and found that he had gone from the house, leaving the street door wide open.

Mr. Pinkerton asked Mrs. Skinner if anything like that had ever happened before. She said that it had not—except for hiding behind the newspaper, of course. Books in the evening and a paper in the morning—that had been his idea of company. Of course he always wanted what he wanted. He was—exacting. But the violence, and leaving the house without a good-bye or an apology, and *leaving the street door open*—that was entirely unlike Skinner.

Mr. Pinkerton nodded agreement. His chief clerk was so meticulously careful both in word and deed. Such behaviour ran contrary to his character. Perhaps Skinner had not been feeling well. Was that the last that Mrs. Skinner had seen of him?

"It was the last I *saw* of him," she answered. But—she went on to say—it was not the last of his insults. She had been waiting for him to come back at eight o'clock in the evening, his usual time unless he was kept late. She had waited until nine, until ten. Finally she had gone to bed, and at last fallen into a nightmare-sleep. In the morning, exhausted, she had come downstairs—and found a bag-shaped purse on the floor of the hall, by the door. It had a string attached to it and appeared to have been lowered through the letter box. Inside the purse were the key of the house and twenty golden guineas.

"The key—so it was left by your husband," Mr. Pinkerton said. "Could the money have been his savings?"

Mrs. Skinner replied that it could not. She did all the saving *that was possible* herself. She had always taken all her husband's wages every week, allowing him a shilling a day for his lunches and travelling expenses. Since they lived at Deptford only six or seven miles away that was generous. It was the arrangement they had come to on their wedding day. No, the money might be stolen for all she knew—stolen from her if no one else—and then given back as a quittance fee. Twenty guineas for twenty-three years of faithful, wifely service! The key meant that he did not intend to come back. In that case she would be destitute. She trusted that Mr. Pinkerton——

Mr. Pinkerton interrupted. The first thing he would do would be to find Skinner. He had the highest opinion of him, both as a clerk and a man. He had known him, he ventured to say, perhaps even longer than his wife had known him. Skinner was a person quite above the ordinary, extremely intelligent, a born organiser, absolutely trustworthy. The mystery would be solved, he promised her.

Mrs. Skinner was momentarily taken aback. But she soon recovered herself. She certainly expected the mystery to be solved. That was why she had come to the office. She had already gone to the Deptford Hospital to make enquiries—and after all she had been through she had needed attention herself. Then she had come to the City—where nobody could tell her the whereabouts of Angel's Way.

Mr. Pinkerton rose imposingly to his feet.

"I intend to start the necessary enquiries immediately, madam. Would you be so kind as to wait in my secretary's room until I can have you escorted to your home? And would you allow me to keep the purse meanwhile?"

G.P., being called in and asked if he had seen the purse being removed from the safe, replied that his impression was that Skinner had taken out a considerably larger bag.

"Is anything missing according to the books?"

"Not as far as I can make out, sir."

"Quite so. I am now going to the police. You, if you please, will take Mrs. Skinner to her home."

The police report when it came was entirely negative. The police had nothing whatever against Skinner and therefore were evidently not interested in him.

But about a week later the senior partner received a registered letter from his chief clerk. It was unheaded and had been posted in Wapping. It enclosed the key of the safe.

It was a formal letter in the impeccable handwriting—thick for the downstrokes, thin for the upstrokes, with artistic twiddles but always perfectly legible—in which the firm's books had been kept for so long. Skinner apologised for not giving proper notice. It was due to what he could only describe as an 'Act of Fate'. He hoped that his sudden departure would not cause inconvenience. He mentioned that for some time he had been training young Roberts to take his place in an emergency. He respectfully brought to the partners' notice one or two outstanding matters of business. If he might venture to make a suggestion it would be best to do so-and-so and so-and-so. Thus, in much the same terms as he had said good night every evening, he said good-bye for ever.

The gossip and speculation about Skinner continued in the office for some time. But nobody can swim for long upon the surface of memory. Roberts, the new chief clerk, re-established a routine among the junior staff. The firm of Pinkerton and Powell continued much as before, and Mrs. Skinner went back to her mother.

2

About eight months later G.P. was thrilled and absorbed by the information that he was definitely to make a tour of the Eastern and tropical trading centres. He would be away more than a year! What an adventure! And the butterflies! Of course he had seen pictures in books, and museum specimens, of those glorious spirits of the day and night which are all colour and have a span of up to eight inches. But he had never allowed himself to believe that he might really catch them, asphyxiate them, and stretch them out on corks with pins.

The senior partner, who had a different idea about the purpose of the tour, told G.P. that he must postpone his start until the arrival in London of Mr. Montgomery, the firm's chief agent in the Far East, who was retiring. Montgomery would be able to brief him on local conditions and tell him what to look out for.

One day a clerk came into G.P.'s little room with the

news that Mr. Montgomery had arrived and was closeted with the partners. G.P. at once began to compile a mental list of intelligent questions. But it was more than two hours before he was summoned to the senior partner's room.

Mr. Pinkerton lounged behind his big leather-topped writing-table. Mr. Powell, if he had been present, had gone. A man with snow-white hair and eyebrows and a round, high-cheekboned face the colour of a dirty lemon sat very upright in one of the two chairs in front of the table.

When Mr. Pinkerton had introduced G.P. to Mr. Montgomery his fingers began to tidy his already tidy desk and he made a few remarks to G.P. about this being a golden opportunity to ask any questions about the Far East and business conditions there.

Then he heaved himself to his feet and said, "I'll leave you two together. I am sure you will excuse me, Montgomery. My wife has a theatre party this evening. But she will be clamouring to make your acquaintance very soon. You will look in tomorrow morning in any case—won't you?—about the annuity. Good night."

Mr. Montgomery bowed slightly. His large, dark eyes followed Mr. Pinkerton out of the room. G.P., who was watching him, noticed that their expression was resentful.

The two men sat down again. There was a silence.

"Did you have a good trip, sir?" G.P. asked.

"Oh, yes. And the firm has kindly booked lodgings for me. The secretary sent my bag there—I have the address written somewhere. The rest can stay at the docks until——"

"But you can't possibly sit in an office and talk to me on your first evening home."

"I have nothing to do," said Montgomery in an expressionless voice. "I am completely at your disposal. But perhaps you are busy."

"Never! I say, sir—please don't think me impertinent —I dare say there are some changes since you were last in town. Would you care to drive round and see the sights? We could talk on the way. Much less cold-blooded than in an empty office."

Montgomery accepted with evident gratitude. Five minutes later they were on top of a bus, in the front seat.

"I do hope it's not too cold, sir," G.P. said. "But I always think this is the best place. When I was a boy I used to imagine I was riding on an elephant through the jungle."

Montgomery looked shocked. "That's no way to talk of dear old London Town . . . Let me see, that shot-tower——"

"The Monument," G.P. corrected.

They passed St. Paul's, Piccadilly Circus, Hyde Park Corner. After his first mistake Montgomery was very cautious in his comments. He talked a lot about 'London Town' and 'the Old Country' in general, but appeared to shy away from particulars. G.P. was puzzled. Suddenly a possible explanation flashed on him. This was the first time that Montgomery had ever been in England and he would rather die than allow it to be known. He was eager but awkward, sensitive and self-conscious. G.P.'s realisation went further. Montgomery knew why the senior partner had not invited him to his house. Half-caste agents were welcome in the office but not in a smart theatre party. To G.P. it seemed too bad. He would never have thought that Pinkerton could be so mean. After all, Montgomery had just retired after heaven knew how many years' service. G.P. felt fiercely protective towards this man three times his own age.

He did his best to put him at his ease and give him a good evening. After their tour they had a drink at the Café Royal, then looked in at a music hall, then had a late meal at the Cheshire Cheese.

"I thought a typical old English inn would be appropriate," G.P. said.

"It is wonderful," Montgomery said, looking round with glowing eyes. He had become quite talkative in his gentle, dreamy way. "You know, Geoffrey, I have looked forward to this evening, the first back home, for a long time, such a long, long time. Then this afternoon it seemed to turn to dust. Now—I couldn't be enjoying myself more. Seeing all the places I've read about so often—to remind myself of them, you know. You are a friend indeed, Geoffrey, although you are young enough to be my grandson."

"Have you grandchildren?" G.P. asked.

"No. No family." Montgomery was sad again. "Somehow I could never manage to find the right girl."

G.P. was searching for a remark which might cheer his guest when Montgomery asked, "What's Pinkerton like to work with—in the same building, I mean?"

"All right. I don't see very much of him, you know. We move in different spheres," G.P. answered, then added with a vague notion that it might be consoling, "I think he was in a bad mood this afternoon. Preoccupied or something."

14

Montgomery suddenly laughed out loud. It was as startling as if the moon had done so.

"Preoccupied! When I showed him that draft for a thousand pounds—I never imagined he did not know the story."

"What story?" G.P. asked.

"About Skinner winning a fortune. He has—a huge one. Wouldn't you think Pinkerton would be pleased? Or at least see the joke? Not a bit of it. He was jealous —or offended. I suppose it hurt that a man he thought he knew inside out—still more that he believed had been slaving for love, worshipping the ground he stood on for the last twenty-five years—had really been scheming and working night and day to get away from him. And the last straw was that when at last he succeeded he did not bother to tell Pinkerton what had happened."

"What did happen?" G.P. asked.

Montgomery said that Skinner had won the jackpot in the Java Sweepstake. The 'Java Swindle' was a quarterly affair in which everybody out East took tickets as a matter of course—a flutter to break the hot monotony of life. Now and then one heard of somebody winning a lesser prize. But the jackpot had been building up for goodness knew how long. Skinner had had a standing order for a few tickets in every sweep throughout the last twenty-five years. He told Montgomery that himself. When he had at last seen his name in the Dutch newspaper to which he subscribed he had at once gone out to claim his prize. The voyage took him months, of course, and he had some trouble in establishing his identity. But having done so and got his money he looked up Montgomery whom he had known in the old days. He entrusted to him a draft for a thousand pounds—with a generous commission added—asking him to buy in England an annuity for Mrs. Skinner. He said he wanted to have his home duties done and finished with for good and all. He did not mean to give another thought to England. That seemed only too true, for apart from one visit to Montgomery he had no contact with any white people. Incredible though it might seem—Montgomery dropped his voice—Skinner evidently preferred natives. He pottered about the bazaars—always in an immaculate white suit, and a big straw hat and dark glasses—buying silks and trinkets and arguing about the price. He paid visits to petty rajahs up-country or along the coast. He saw the sights like any tourist, when he might have painted the whole place vermilion and then gone home to the Old Country to live like a duke! Montgomery's own private dream had always been to go back to the Old Country when he retired, to buy a small place and end his days like a gentle-man. And there was Skinner, only about forty-five, strong and healthy and clear enough in the head from all accounts, preferring the East. It was not as if he could have happy memories of those parts.

G.P. enquired about these memories and the earlier reference to the old days. He was told that a quarter of a century before, Pinkerton had been sent by his father on much the same tour that G.P. was to make. But being the son of the head of the firm he had been given a secretary —Skinner, the promising young clerk. Pinkerton, being a wild young spark in those days——

Montgomery suddenly broke off. He did not think he ought to say any more. But gradually he was persuaded. After all he was no longer a member of the firm and had not been treated as well as he might have been on retirement.

In those days—Montgomery went on in a whisper—Pinkerton was more interested in the bright lights and all that sort of thing than in the firm's affairs. He was not going to waste a world cruise on business, not when he had a reliable secretary to do the work. Of course he had to put in an appearance in the big places—Singapore and Macassar and Rangoon and so on. He didn't mind that. But he sent Skinner off in the schooner to do the rough jobs while he enjoyed himself for weeks and months together. And when Skinner came back with the reports, Pinkerton signed them. You could hardly credit it, but it was true. Skinner had never been allowed one day free to enjoy himself. Pinkerton said he didn't know how to! But that was when Skinner had started buying tickets in the Java Sweep. And now he was a millionaire.

"Do you think I might come across him?" G.P. asked.

"You might. But I've no idea what he meant to do. He can't keep on sightseeing for ever.

3

G.P. was enraptured by the East—the colours, the smells, the fantastic exaggerations in animal and vegetable life, the violence of the sunshine, the gentle other-worldness of the night, the ports, the shipping, the buildings, the people, their queer music, the feeling that riches, romance and death were just around the corner, the mystery, the spell. He lived in a state of mental intoxication, in an exciting dream.

He did not come across Skinner in the Archipelago. Nor did he hear much about him. Without anyone to help him he was extremely busy, and any spare time he had was spent in solitary explorations or in pursuit of his hobby rather than in social surroundings. But also the white residents between Java and Japan appeared to have grown tired of speculating on what Skinner was up to. There was only one definite piece of information. He had bought the *Southern Cross*, a brig of one hundred and sixty tons. She had formerly been used for general trading and by one of her owners as a transport for native pilgrims. There was no information on what Skinner intended to use her for. He had manned her entirely with Malayans. As everybody knew, the men of the shallow seas were born seamen. But an inexperienced European might have had a white mate or sailing master. Skinner did not. And a peculiarity which a certain port officer who had been on board had commented upon was that all the crew were old—wrinkled old monkeys long past their prime.

Since commissioning the *Southern Cross* Skinner had been heard of here and there. But nobody knew what he was up to because he seemed to make a point of avoiding his own race.

That was all G.P. learned before he sailed further eastward to begin the most exacting part of his educational tour. He visited the widely scattered Pacific Ocean trading centres, working under the agents and learning all there was to know about the business. This occupied him for almost a year. Then he turned back westward on his return journey.

It was at a lonely station in the Solomon Islands, where the only form of entertainment was the swapping of yarns between the sea captains who called there, that G.P. heard the following story.

The yawl *Peregrine* was beating into Torres Strait from the westward, Joe Page and his son Mike in the cockpit. As they cleared Booby Island there came into their view a two-masted vessel under full sail. She lay some three miles off on their starboard bow and at about an equal distance from the north shore of the island. The two men —Joe with a face like a fist and eyes like diamond rings, Mike young and eager—looked intently at the strange craft.

After a silent minute Mike exclaimed, "She's not moving!"

"Because she's on the reef," said Joe.

It was not extraordinary that a ship should run into trouble in those waters. The danger of the Strait was acknowledged by the maintenance in a cave on Booby Island of a supply of stores for the use of shipwrecked mariners. Joe Page had known several ships come to grief during his seven years in the area. He was a pearler, an Australian, a successful man in his line of business. He found the *Peregrine* a handy little vessel for dodging about among the many rocks and islands as he made his constant round of visits to his various fishing craft.

"Tom!" Joe Page shouted.

A well-made native with a shockingly ugly face came up from the galley where he had been preparing breakfast.

Joe told him to fetch the telescope. He passed the helm to Mike and studied the wreck long and carefully. She was a brigantine, of something over two hundred tons,

Joe guessed. She must have run hard and fast on to the reef for she was as steady among the waves as if she had been in dock. But there seemed to be no damage above the water line. This did not surprise him, for since he had last passed Booby Island four days previously the trade winds had been in a gentle mood. A boat hung from its davits, suggesting that the people were still aboard although no one was on deck. No flag was flying.

"We'll find out," Joe said—an omnibus answer to the questions which his son had been asking during the last few minutes.

Half an hour later the *Peregrine* was hove-to at a safe distance from the reef. They hailed but received no answer. Joe ordered Tom to take the helm while he and Mike rowed over in the dinghy to the brigantine. They hailed her again but still received no answer. On her square stern where there might have been a name there was none. Joe's quick eyes noticed that the paint was blotchy as if part of the stern had been repainted, but he made no comment. He signed to Mike to row round to the bow. They climbed on board.

At once they saw much litter and disorder. A trail of native garments and other personal belongings led to the forecastle where chests stood empty or part empty. The store and galley were in similar disorder as if they had been quickly rifled. There was a quantity of rice grains strewn about. Everything suggested a hurried abandonment of the ship.

"But how?" asked Mike, pointing to the boat hanging from the davits.

"I guess they had another, a bigger one," his father

said, and showed the lashings which might have held a long-boat to the deck.

In contrast to the mess forward, the saloon—a big, airy room—was in good order. And the captain's cabin was as tidy as could be. There were a number of English books, including an almanac and works on navigation and seamanship. European suits, shirts and ties were stowed away neatly in the locker. There was a London-made watch which had stopped at a quarter past four.

"He left quietly enough," Mike said.

Joe, his face as expressionless as an undertaker's, nodded. He was looking for the ship's papers. He failed to find them, or anything to give a hint as to the brigantine's identity. The log was gone. But the slate on which notes are made until they can be entered in the log book was in its place. It was headed '29th'. (The date of the day being described was 26th June.) Below was written, "Noon. A minute above the line." Below there was a single word in block capitals—'ARRIVED!'

Joe told his son to return to the *Peregrine* and send Tom over in his place. When Tom came aboard the brigantine he sniffed about like a dog in a strange house.

"Your people?" Tom asked.

Tom shook his head vigorously.

"Where they go, Tom?" Joe pointed at the land to the southward.

Tom said no. One of the pearlers which were scattered along the Australian coast would have seen them, or news of them would have been brought from the interior. No strangers could pass unremarked.

Joe Page turned and looked northward at the mountains of New Guinea. He had no one to give him information there. He had an idea that strangers were not welcome thereabouts, except maybe on the menu. Beyond New Guinea lay open ocean, and in the direction where the ship had been heading the complex of islands large and small which make up the Malay Archipelago.

Joe and Tom left the brigantine and rowed back to join Mike in the *Peregrine*. They sailed to the cave on Booby Island. It had always been Joe's habit to visit this store fairly frequently, to add something to the case of provisions and also to see if there were a letter for him. For the cave was maintained not only as a refuge for castaways but also as an unofficial post office, used mainly by whalers, but occasionally by coastal craft.

The stores had not been touched. Nor was there any note or letter. No sailing master using the Torres Strait was likely to be unaware of that cave. But these shipwrecked mariners had not made use of it, even to leave information of their plight.

Joe Page next visited the nearest of his pearlers. He took off two men, carried them to the brigantine and instructed them to guard her. Bad weather was not likely at that season. She would sit safely enough where she was, he thought, until he had gathered his fleet and got her off. If her skipper and crew did not want her, he did.

Before leaving he made a final tour of the vessel. He convinced himself that the name had been obliterated from the stern. A close examination of the rigging suggested that the main mast had once been square rigged, like the foremast, not fore-and-aft rigged as it was. This would radically have altered the appearance of the vessel.

In the forecastle, galley and store he found nothing new. There was no cargo. In fact the cargo space appeared to have been used mainly for accommodation.

The captain's cabin was as neatly uninformative as before. Joe Page went into the saloon, sat down and mopped his face and neck.

Mike joined him. All morning the young man had been propounding a string of explanatory theories, more or less bloodthirsty. Now he said, "The strongest proof of dirty work is the way they have removed all trace of the ship's name——"

He broke off, looking at his father, whose gaze was fixed upon something on the wall of the saloon. It was a heraldic shield carrying a design of twelve stars arranged in the form of a cross.

Mike looked blankly at it, and then the light of excitement came into his eyes.

"It's the ship's crest. It could stand for her name. Natives wouldn't know. They call the Cross something else, I suppose. Gee! What do you think?"

"I guess——" Joe said.

"What?"

"I guess I dunno. But it don't alter the value of the salvage."

Chapter Two

"Was it Skinner's ship?" someone asked G.P.

"Yes, yes, of course," my grandparent answered. "But the ship doesn't matter. It was the dream she had been bound on. The Malay seamen did not share Skinner's dream. How could they? They were afraid and tried to get home."

I remember as a young man hearing him saying that and wondering what he meant. He sat at the head of the table, smiling an old man's smile, while the port went round and we waited for him to go on talking. He did not like being interrupted. He was a wonderful host, but autocratic. At last he went on:

"We each dream of a different heaven. I don't mean the one that comes to some of us after death. That's fixed and settled one way or the other. I mean the type of life we would lead and the sort of people we would be if we had an absolutely free choice—a supernaturally free choice. That particular heaven is created in secret by our own imagination. I don't suppose you would tell me about yours. You would be afraid of being laughed at. So would I. We know perfectly well that it is not practical, but we keep it carefully packed away in the back of our minds because it is an escape from the discomforts of reality to dream about it now and then.

"One person in a million is not content to dream. He plans. At last he throws everything to the winds and goes bald-headed for his particular heaven. It's a dangerous

24

thing to do. But danger is the last thing to stop him. Skinner was like that. And Ronald Mackintosh was like that. You haven't heard of Ronald yet. He was a very different type from Skinner, so of course his choice of heaven was as different as could be. But he was the same one-in-a-million sort which risks everything and stops at nothing to turn a dream into reality. And it so happens that I can tell you the whole story, so I will."

Chapter Three

Rain was coming down with dreary purposefulness as if it meant to go on for ever. Individual drops were not distinguishable. The soaking atmosphere descended obliquely to the saturated ground where it wriggled in rivulets which converged and made every sheep-track into a stream. Through the grey haze, rocks and heather slopes and a few stunted pines with their shoulders hunched against the prevailing wind were dimly visible.

A young man, his face sun-tanned to a shade not far from black, forged steadily through the rain. His good new coat was wrapped tightly round him. His head was for the most part down, but now and then he raised it to look about. He was following a cart-track beside a burn, a wild little river the colour of beer except where it foamed over rocks. Here and there it had flooded the path so that it was necessary to make a detour through wet bracken.

He skirted the shore of a small loch. Near the lower end was a boat shed and a living house, but with no smoke rising from it. The young man pressed on beside the burn which was now noticeably larger than before.

A mile farther on, the hurrying river and the man rounded a little hill and came in view of the sea loch with

26

yellow weed on the tidal strip. The narrow estuary wound between hills whose tops were in the cloud. In the water were rocky islets like half-submerged wrecks over which waves were breaking. But the man's eyes were on the cluster of small houses which grew like mushrooms near the shore.

At the head of the sea loch was a boat-building yard, a shed and stocks on which was set a keel and skeleton of ribs. The young man recognised the embryo of a Loch Corron cutter—fishing vessels once famous all along the coast for their seaworthiness and ease in handling. But no one was working on this unfinished craft, and there was no one in the yard. The young man walked on, more slowly.

As he approached the houses a dog barked. A man on some domestic errand paused, stared and then came forward. Other men appeared at his call. They surrounded the newcomer and spoke with him for some minutes, oblivious of the rain. Two of them left the group and went into the largest of the houses. Later one of them reappeared at the door and beckoned. The newcomer went in and embraced an old woman who sat bowed forward in her chair beside a spinning-wheel. An ancient sheep dog rose, sniffed and shivered. The old woman gripped the arms of her chair as a bird grips a bough. The name of God was murmured. For a while there was much emotion in the simple room though little visible sign of it.

The newcomer was Ronald Mackintosh, the third in age of the widow's five sons. It was the eldest, Duncan, and the second, Alexander, who had gone first into the house to bring their mother gently to the realisation that

Ron was not dead as they had been informed but alive and well and just outside the door.

Ronald was not surprised that his two younger brothers were not there to welcome him. Before his father died, and therefore before he himself had gone to sea, Angus and Rory had been sent to a forestry estate on the east coast, above Inverness, because even then there had not been work enough for everyone at Corron.

The neighbours left the family in peace to shake down on their own. The white-haired woman and her three men sat looking at each other and not talking much at first. But even in their slowly spoken and scant conversation a stranger would have noticed how far above the rest of his family was Ronald both in manner and the turn of phrase. For Ronald was the clever one who in the Highland tradition had been early singled out to be given the best possible chance in life at the expense of all the rest. His brothers had uncomplainingly gone without many things, even good food, to aid his education. His father, the village schoolmaster, had started this education. Then Ronald had gone on to a much larger school and finally, with a scholarship, to Oxford University.

He had just completed his first year there when his father died. His family told him that they would do anything to keep him at the university until he had taken his degree. But he felt like a traveller who had suddenly become uncertain whether he was on the right road. His father had, virtually, been the only source of actual money. Suppose the others could somehow scrape and save enough to maintain him as a student of law, could he accept it? He decided that he could not. Even when he had his degree the money which his family so urgently needed

28

would still be a long way off. He resolved to leave the university and to take a short-cut to fortune. He had a call, an instinctive feeling that he knew how to succeed.

His brothers had found it difficult to forgive him for throwing away so much that they had helped to give. His mother, already saddened, was almost broken-hearted. But Ronald had stubbornly persisted in his resolve. He had gone to sea. They had heard little from him for eight years and nothing after that. Then they had received a letter from a Captain Matthews stating that he had been drowned. His few effects had arrived later. His brother Alexander was still wearing his coat.

And here he was, a picture of health and self-confidence. What had he brought back? They did not ask him and he did not tell them during that first conversation. Instead he asked the questions—about life at Corron. The voices which answered him were gentle, lilting. His brothers were grave-mannered, steady-eyed, and careful of their words as of their pennies. Life was harder than ever. Bad weather had spoiled the growing crops and prevented the hay from drying. Many cattle had had to be slaughtered during the winter. Worst of all, the new yards of the Clyde had progressively during the last ten years been robbing Corron of shipbuilding orders. They had appealed to their Member of Parliament, but to no better effect than to be told that they were victims of progress.

Although his brothers gave no hint of criticism, Ronald felt every word as a charge against himself who might by this time have been a man of position. The wind made a mournful background to their talk and rain dripped from the eaves. Night came slowly down without a sign of sunset.

29

Ronald went out and made a tour of the village, visiting old friends and relations. He invited a few of these to the house. Later in the evening about a dozen men and women came into the old lady's sitting-room. She had little to offer them by way of refreshment. They all knew they were gathered for a family conclave, not a party for a prodigal. A single lamp burned on the table. A peat fire glowed, giving out its musky odour to mix with the sharper smell of damp tweeds. The wind was still upon its mournful journey and the fire spat when rain came down the chimney.

Ronald in a quiet voice began the record of the missing years.

He said that he became a sailor because that is the only way to travel without money. But he was not merely adventuring upon the sea. He tried the gold-fields of Australia, the plantations of the West Indies. Following a rumour of silver he explored the Andes. He found back-breaking labour, fever, hunger, thirst, hard knocks—but not a fortune.

"What does a fisherman do when he catches nothing?" Ronald asked of the quiet people in the dim-lit room.

Nobody answered.

"He goes on fishing—does he not?" he said. "So did I. I could not return home with an empty basket. But I'll spare you the disappointments—until it seemed that God had forsaken me, a sick man in Valparaiso. I was leaving the door of the hospital, cured but penniless, when I saw a group of British sailors carrying a man in on a litter. I never knew his name, but in twenty seconds I learned enough to take his place.

"I found myself aboard the research ship, *Swan*. She

was bound round the world with a party of four scientists, a Professor Browning and three young assistants who were making surveys—botanical, zoological, geological—of the least known points of land upon this sphere. At once I felt that God still held the door ajar. I had been doubtful during my sickness whether I ought to go to sea again. I had learned that merchant ships follow lanes very much as carriages do, and once a man has sailed about for a few years he finds himself repeating his old journeys. But the *Swan* had a roving commission to discover nature's secrets.

"I became very friendly with the scientists, especially with Browning who held a professorship at Oxford although he had not been there when I was up. On the mid-ocean rocks and the wild points of land where the *Swan* put in for as long as the weather allowed, they depended a great deal on the help the crew gave them in making their collections and surveys. The professor found me readier and, he said, more able to do what he wanted than the other sailors—who were for ever grumbling that there was no grog-shop 'for a bit of fun'. Captain Matthews, who looked upon the scientists as moderately harmless lunatics for whose safety and satisfaction he was responsible, was pleased enough. As for me, it was like water after a drought to hear intelligent conversation again. They took nothing for granted, those men. How was it formed, the rock that we were standing on—from the skeletons of millions upon millions of sea creatures or an eruption from the cauldron of the world's interior? This lonely island, had it been thrust up by a contortion of the cooling crust or split away from the nearest continent? They studied the evidence. The plants, the animals— where was there similar life? To what extent could seeds

31

and living creatures be transported in the roots of drifting tree-trunks or by birds? There was no blasphemy in their questioning, quite the reverse. They were fascinated by the intricate details of God's plan which the book of Genesis finds no room for."

Ronald paused. There was a stir of interest among his audience. Their native intelligence and their Celtic imagination were his own. Most of them had been educated by his father, a dedicated and inspired teacher. Also there was Bruce, the story-teller of Corron, who until he had lost an arm twenty years before had been first mate and chief harpooner on a whaler.

"I need not describe tropic oceans, storms, whales, blinding sunlight, flying fish and albatrosses," Ronald said. "You have maybe heard even more about them than I have seen these last ten years."

There was a murmur of amusement and the deep laugh of old Bruce himself.

"I was not gallivanting with science any more than I had been adventuring for its own sake. While I carried specimens for the scientists I was using my eyes, looking for something of practical value. But always if there were coconuts there were people making copra. Whatever was of value was already being worked. I seemed always too late. I can't tell you of all the places we visited during ten months of voyaging, but I want to describe one island— Ecalpemos."

"And where might that be?" Bruce asked.

"In the middle of an ocean. It's an island smaller than Arran. It must be one of the most remote spots of land in the whole world."

"Ecalpemos——?"

32

"That is my name for it and it will do for the present, back to front though it may be."

"You are mighty secretive," Bruce grumbled.

"Is it unknown?" Alexander asked.

"It is uninhabited, Sandy. I will give you the description I had of it before I saw it. There was said to be no record of anybody ever landing on it—and for a good reason. But it was not unknown. It was discovered some time before 1680, for it appeared on a Dutch chart of that date. It had been sighted several times since then, in the year 1777 by Captain Cook. It was described in the pilot book as being shaped like a shoe, wider at the two ends than in the middle—about fifteen miles long, three or four miles wide near the two ends and perhaps three miles across in the middle. It was low-lying except for a central sharp-pointed mountain. The island was entirely girdled by cliffs which forbade any attempt at landing. Nor was there a safe anchorage, for the island, being set lengthwise to the prevailing wind, offered a minimum of shelter. The water was extremely deep right up to the cliffs.

"I learned this from the scientists during the last long passage. They wanted to examine Ecalpemos because it might prove to be the top of a mountain rising steeply from the ocean bed and just breaking the surface—a thing much rarer than a coral island.

"We sighted it one evening. It was bleak as a fortress, its cliff walls surmounted by a steep slope covered with scrub. But the mountain was sharp and tall as Ailsa Craig. What we could see of it was white as snow, but it was half hidden by cloud. As we approached we realised that this wreathing cloud was formed of innumerable birds. The sun touched the sea. The birds went to roost.

For a few minutes the mountain blazed with every colour there is. Then it went out. But in the dim moonlight we were conscious of the roaring of the waves, angry at this obstructing rock after thousands of free ocean miles.

"We lay off for the night. I was on deck at first light, looking at the island. During the long weeks of our passage out of sight of all land it had been the main subject of conversation. But it was not much to look at even in the beauty of dawn except for the mountain, now rosy in colour, and the birds which were wheeling and twisting, billowing out and regrouping, making the air alive.

"The scientists joined me, with telescopes. They studied the island long and carefully. As usual they opened my eyes. The cliffs must be of soft rock, they said, for they had been undercut by the waves. The scrub slope above the cliffs ended in a rocky rim where nothing grew, presumably because of the wind. It was as even in height as is the top of a slipper. Its line was only broken by the mountain spire which went shooting up a thousand feet or more. The geologist said that the mountain must be of much harder rock, almost certainly volcanic, possibly basalt. It had survived comparatively well although the softer rock of the island had been eroded away.

"But basalt is black," I said, feeling a catch at my heart as I thought of the Hebrides.

Professor Browning laughed. "This has been painted by the birds," he said.

I asked whether the seeds of the scrub we could see must have been carried by birds. The Professor answered that it might be so, but also it was possible that the island had once been much larger and connected with other land. "You would not recognise a map of this world of a few

34

million years ago," he said. "Who knows? We might find a most interesting fauna as well as flora in the more sheltered parts."

"Still talking of the island while the kedgeree was cooking, one of the young scientists pointed out that since the sharp mountain was the only thing which broke the outline of the coastal rim, the rest of the island must either be flat or indented like a bowl. If a bowl it would fit in with his volcanic theory. It might be the remains of a crater.

"I went up to the top of the mast. But I just could not see over the coastal rim. I felt like a child shut out of a walled garden and unable to look into it even by climbing a tree.

"The next blow was that I was not named for the landing party. I suspect that Captain Matthews thought I was a little above myself, being so friendly with the scientists. But Professor Browning told me afterwards that he impressed on him I was just the man for a quick raid which was the best that could be hoped for. At the last moment I was called into the whale-boat. Browning was a difficult man to say no to—a big, impressive figure.

"None the less it was the most disappointing day of my life. We sailed or rowed right round the island, but found no place where the captain would try to land. So the scientists had to be content with what they could discover from the boat. We could get no bottom with the lead. The cliffs were of limestone. They were about a hundred feet high. Not only had they been undercut by the ceaseless nagging of the sea, but in places there were caves. When the rollers drove into these they trapped the air." Ronald clapped his cupped hands. "The noise was something like that but ten thousand times more loud. Elsewhere the waves licked along the rocks and the spray rose high into the air as bonfire smoke. And all the time the whale-boat was rising and falling ten feet or more as the swell passed under her. No one blamed the captain for keeping well out from the cliffs.

"We travelled the length of the south side first, then rounded the heel of the island and started along the northern side. The island was the shape of a shoe as the old navigator had said. The northern side was the inner side. The coast made a concave line for two-thirds of the distance. One can't describe it as a bay—rather as a wide indentation. We rowed straight across. But my eye was caught by something strange in the behaviour of the waves near the head of this indentation. Looking carefully it seemed to me that there was a crack in the cliff. It was impossible to be certain at that distance. But you know I have always been able to trust my eyes and it seemed to me there might be a sheltered cove, however small. I pointed it out and suggested that we ought to go in and examine it.

"The captain told me briefly—and very clearly—that he could manage without my advice. So I rowed on in silence.

"On the way back to the *Swan* a strange thing happened. We had not been able to identify any of the birds for certain. From close in they were hidden by the cliff, and from further out they were too distant. But as we turned away from the island a little white tern came skimming after us. It was the most delicately lovely bird I ever saw. It hovered motionless, close before my face, looking at me steadily with its large black eye. Just as we reached the

36

ship it gave me a wink—and then away it darted and was lost in the great cloud of birds.

"I was in need of something like that to cheer me, for I had just heard the captain say that since a landing was out of the question we would sail next morning. He would have been away at once except that the carpenter had taken the opportunity to do some work on the rudder and was not finished yet.

"I could not go below that night. I leaned on the rail and looked at the island. Even under the moon its fortress cliffs were not beautiful. But something told me that I ought to look at whatever lay behind them. What had told me? I believed it was that bird with the all-knowing eye which had studied me carefully, read my heart's secret, and given me that sign—a wink."

One of the listeners murmured something and several of the men stirred in their chairs. Behind the roughest exterior the true Highlander hides poetry and a belief in the supernatural.

Ronald went on. "In the small hours of the morning temptation came to me—in such a plausible form! If I could get ashore for an hour or two and collect some plants and stones and insects—I knew the sort of thing to look for—the scientists would be so pleased that the captain could not punish me severely. And—the important thing —I would be able to look beyond the coastal rim at what nobody had ever seen. Whatever I found or did not find I would not be haunted for the rest of my life by the spectre of a lost opportunity.

"The *Swan* lay peacefully hove-to. When my watch was done the relieving watch came sleepily on deck. They did not see me in the shadow of one of the boats. They were

37

taking little notice of anything, for it was a calm night. The carpenter's gig still trailed astern, waiting for him to finish his job at first light. I was sure that I had seen a hole in the defences of the island and that I would have a good chance of getting ashore there. The more I thought about it the more was I certain that the tern had brought me a message, an order.

"The moon has never taken so long to set. But directly it went below the sea I slid down the rope into the gig and cut her loose. I let her drift until I could scarcely make out the *Swan* and was certain that the watch could not see me even if they were looking. Then I took to the oars and rowed over the hills and valleys of the swell in the direction of the thundering waves.

"I located the crack. It was a crack right enough. I waited for enough light to see what lay behind. I knew that my landing would have to be done smartly or not at all, for the carpenter would miss his gig and when the sun rose I would be spotted from the ship unless I were over the coastal rim.

"The light came flooding and I could see. Some tremendous shock had split off a portion of the cliff as large as a big house and tumbled it forward, away from the rest. There was a breach in the defences about as wide as a gate, and beyond a tiny cove with a sloping shore. The waves were sweeping across the narrow entrance and eddying back from the other side.

"I set the gig at it before I had time to lose my nerve. I would have done better to wait and get frightened and work out the drift more carefully. I rowed as hard as I could to keep steerage-way, but of course I had my back to the trouble.

38

"The gig was swept into the lee side of the entrance. The wave then lifted her and banged her against an overhang. Luckily it was the bow that got stoved in and not my head. Down came the gig with her timbers splitting apart, and I was thrown out.

"I swam. The eddies snatched at me. Then I was in calm water. I reached the shore and waded on to a shelving beach. I saw the gig very low in the water, waltzing in slow circles and bumping against the sides of the entrance. Then the current took her by the hand and led her out and beyond my sight into the troughs of the swell.

" 'If I can't go back I must go on,' I thought. The cracking of the cliff had formed a rough stairway of broken blocks. I climbed the hundred feet of cliff quite easily. I reached the scrub slope and began to push my way through bushes as twisted and entangled as a negro's hair. I paused for breath and looked back. When I stood upright I was taller than the scrub bushes. Even from the height I'd gained I could not see the gig. She had gone for good. But I was not afraid of becoming a castaway. I had nothing with which to light a signal fire. But I could wave from the rim. My fear was of another sort—of punishment and of the fool that I would look. My mind was not working very clearly. It clung to something it remembered. I started collecting at once—twig after twig of the scrub, although they were all the same, stones, anything.

"I reached the rim. I pushed my way a few paces through the prickly scrub which grew on the inland side of the rim. Then I halted, dropping my useless burden. I don't know what I had expected—not what I saw.

"Close on my left was the mountain. It shut off the eastern two-thirds of the island—the toe end—from my sight. I could not in that first glimpse see any way of passing it, for its northern buttress was rooted in the cliff. But what held my eyes was the view directly in front of me and to the right. I saw an almost symmetrical bowl with a lake at the bottom of it. The lake was blue and smooth. The sides of the bowl were a luxuriant green. What broke the symmetry was the mountain sprouting up on the left side of the lake, cutting it off from the rest of the island. But the bowl below me was lovely beyond words compared with the hostile barrenness of the aspect from the sea. I had never seen anything so peaceful and inviting.

"Suddenly I heard a gun. I fell flat as if the ball had knocked my head off.

"As I lay there I wondered at myself. Not for a fraction of a second had I thought of deserting. I could scarcely have been worse-equipped. I was in shirt and trousers, with only a knife and a handkerchief in my pocket. Yet as soon as the ship called me I dropped to the ground in case any part of me might still be visible above the rim. Throughout all my wanderings I had been practical. I had searched for wealth. But suddenly I had acted on impulse like a wild youth who falls in love at first sight.

"While I lay there with my sensible side scolding at me I heard a noise which made my skin contract. It sounded like the internal gurgling and rumblings of some enormous animal, and it was quite close. But even that did not shift me. What did was a second report of gunfire, from much closer than before. A new fear drove out the other.

Captain Matthews might be sending a landing party after all. I knew how angry he could become, and anger affects judgment. I crawled back to the rim and peeped between the rocks.

"There was no ship's boat in the water. But the *Swan* was being worked to windward, at every other tack coming within a cable's length of the cliff. I could sense the captain's fury in the way that she was being handled. She was bristling with telescopes, and every sailor in every spare moment was staring towards the island under a shading hand. I could recognise my chums, and the captain's scarlet face, and the officers, and the scientists— the scientists who could read the history of an island just by looking at it. It seemed a wonder they could not spot me.

"I crawled backwards until I was a fathom or so below the rim. There was no need to keep the ship in view to know where she was, for she continued to fire her gun at short intervals. All the time it seemed as if the island were ablaze from the wreathing smoke of birds. They would begin to settle—and then the next shot would send them billowing up again.

"The *Swan* rounded the windward point, the Heel, and ran down upon the southern side. A couple of hours later she had reached the Toe and was beating up to where she had started on the northern side. She came abreast of the cove. Again I felt the grip of fear. I saw her turned into the wind, and a boat lowered. The sailors pulled off briskly. They came alongside something. I could distinguish nothing except a slight difference in the surface of the water, but it must have been the gig, awash. They made the thing fast and fished about in it. They pulled

41

out what could have been a drowned dog, but which I guessed was my coat. They rowed slowly back to the ship.

"Then I saw something happen aboard the *Swan*. The ensign was dipped. That's a fine compliment to a dead sailor.

"When next I looked the *Swan* was sailing away. I watched her until first her hull and finally her topsails went over the curve of the world and out of sight. By then it was almost sunset. Only then did I stand up on the crest of the rim and turn about and wonder what I could do for myself."

2

"I had a bad night. I was hungry and cold and I had no means of making fire. My bed was a steep slope, knotty with roots. But what kept me awake were the rumbling-gurgling noises which had scared me even during the day. It sounded as if the huge prehistoric creature I had already imagined had a stomach as empty as mine. In that case my prospects were poor if he should find me.

"I came suddenly to myself when the sun jumped out of the sea. I could only have slept for a very short time—for I had seen the light beginning to grow—but so deeply that for a minute I did not know where I was.

"A little brown bird was sitting on my chest. His tail stuck straight up in the air, and he turned his head continually from side to side as if his two eyes could not agree on what they were seeing. He gave me a little peck as if to see what I was made of, and then away he went chirruping like a child that's found treasure. In a minute he was back with a score of little pals who went peeping and pecking all over me as robins do on a bit of ground a man is digging.

"There came the prehistoric snort and gurgle. The little birds took no notice. I became ashamed of my fears and crawled off to investigate——" Ronald laughed. "I was spurted in the face with fine spray. My enemy was a blow-hole. I remembered the caves we had seen from the sea. Some of them have a vent in the roof through which spray is ejected when a wave drives in. We had not heard this from the ship because of the noise of breakers between.

"That calmed my fears but not my hunger. I wanted to get down to the lake where I supposed I might catch fish or find some vegetable thing to eat. The only obstacle in my way was the entanglement of thorny scrub which grew as high up on the inside of the rim as on the outer. But I was so tired and weak it seemed impossible to force a way through. I might have given up if I had not come upon the last thing I expected—a track."

"An animal track?" someone asked.

"This was much wider than any I had ever seen. You know how narrow is a sheep or deer track—not more than a foot wide. This was quite three feet across and so well beaten down that nothing grew on it even in a place where vegetation sprouted with wild exuberance. But in the thickets it was only clear for three feet above the track. I crawled through a tunnel, wondering who or what could have made such a track. Then I met one of the road-builders. It was a giant tortoise. He must have weighed three or four times as much as I did and he looked as old as the world. We stared at each other for a moment. Then, suddenly, he withdrew his head and feet and

43

flopped down on the ground. I climbed over the top of him and we continued on our different ways.

"The jungle-thick zone was of no great width. I was soon in open forest where I could walk freely. This in turn gave place, near the shores of the lake, to coconut palms, banana, orange and breadfruit trees, vines, pineapples, guavas and a number of other useful trees and shrubs, some of them in fruit. Why this rich vegetation flourished was clear enough, for the ground flattened out near the lake and all the rain which fell on the inner sides of the bowl drained slowly through it, now and then breaking the surface as a spring. But how such a variety came to be there at all puzzled me until I thought of the great multitude of birds, many species of which must go away yearly on their long migrations and return with the seeds of the luscious fruits they have fed on in their crops or stomachs, or perhaps in some cases on their feet. I could almost hear the scientists lecturing me!

"I used the word garden. But you must not get a picture of anything orderly. Each species struggled with the others for existence, and I suppose conquered where the ground happened to suit it better than its adversaries.

"I did not bother my head with such questions then, as you can imagine. I picked myself as much fruit as I could eat, and then lay down to sleep in the shade of a banana tree. I woke in the evening, reached a hand up for my supper, and slept again. When morning came I bathed in the lake, which to my great surprise was salt. I floated on my back and watched the birds rejoicing like a host of angels against the clouds of dawn. Then I came ashore, dried in the sunshine, and had the most refreshing breakfast a man could wish.

"I could have continued that idle life indefinitely. I had no fire, but one misses cooking much less in a hot climate. In the season I used occasionally to fry eggs on a rock in the sun, and I dried the fish I caught in the shallows. But I spent no time in the kitchen. With no tools other than a knife I never attempted to make a shelter. I soon had no clothes—and felt better without them. We used to enjoy *Robinson Crusoe* as children. You remember? What a lot of time that man wasted on tailoring and building and farming, trying to turn Eden into Civilisation.

"I will tell you of the explorations which were my whole occupation. My first surprising discovery, as I have said, was that the lake was salt. I could not think at first how this might be. Then I calculated that its surface must be the same as that of the ocean. And it rose and fell with the tide. I remembered the blowholes, some of which were well inland. Evidently one or more of the caves pierced right through the sides of the island. In fact if there was a big storm outside its ghost shimmered on the surface of the lake. So the lake was really a lagoon, connected with the ocean.

"I wandered all over the island. The tortoise tracks were very useful. I never had to cut a path. The strange animals drink at the springs, plunging their heads right under water. Then they turn about and march up to the rim. I suppose they find some food there to their taste, but I often saw them standing like armoured sentries among the battlements of rock. When the period of their watch is done—it may be of several days' duration—they hurry down towards the water again with outstretched necks while the relieving guard march stolidly uphill.

45

"It was by following the tortoise tracks that I found my way past the sides of the mountain to visit the other half of the island. Otherwise it would be quite an awkward scramble. But those great beasts are wonderful engineers.

"What I named the Toe of the island is even more fertile and beautiful than the Heel, where the lagoon is. Outside the rainy season the mountain attracts occasional thunder-storms which keep the whole island green. But the Toe has the greater variety of fruits—a lot of coconut palms, for instance—and quantities of flowers, flowering shrubs and creepers. Besides, that part is full of grottoes and springs and glades. There is a great cave with an underground lake. There are fairy-fashioned stalactites and stalagmites. I was happy dreaming of how I would some day show you these marvels. It was always my dream to bring you some day to Ecalpemos. I used to think of you at Corron, struggling from dawn to darkness among rocks and rain while I was in the sunlight, where there was earth in which anything will grow, and rich pasturage. The wild turkeys which abound there are as fine as any I ever saw in an expensive shop at Christmas time. But the little birds, the birds of bright plumage, and the swift-flying birds! They were my friends. They were the admirers or critics of everything I did. They were absolutely tame—no need of a bribe of food if I wanted to feel their child-like grip on my fingers.

"The monkeys were my friends too, although mighty mischievous ones, always up to trouble. They would make you laugh. They *will*! I always dreamed of bringing you to the island. But at first it seemed completely unpractical. Even if I ever got home again I would have no money. And to bring a shipload of pioneers all the way from Scotland would need a powerful lot of money. How can a man make his fortune in an uninhabited island, the loneliest in the world?

"I'm afraid the moral of this story is a bad one, for it was greed that showed me the way. Every morning and evening I had taken a swim in the lagoon. I had learned to dive like a duck in the clear water. It was beautiful and cool down there among the multi-coloured fishes, shells and polyps. Also it was safe, for whatever the connection with the ocean might be, the sharks had not found it or could not use it.

"I noticed oysters. By their plainness they stood out from the many pretty things. It struck me that here was a raw flesh that I might eat with relish. I duck-dived and at last succeeded in getting down to the bottom and bringing up one, about the size of a soup plate. I took it ashore and opened it with my knife. At the last moment I had qualms. There was an R in the month. But I was in the southern hemisphere. I wondered if that reversed the rule. However I persisted. It was not very good. In fact it nearly made me sick. However I stuck to eating oysters and got quite used to them. I gulped them down, not looking at the slimy flesh—until one day my teeth grated on something and I spat out a pearl as big as a pea.

"That altered the way I spent my days! I dived for oysters from morning till night. But I found it extremely exhausting, and unprofitable. Most of the shells were in water which was too deep for me. I needed some craft that would carry a stone heavy enough to weight me down. I knew of a grove of tall bamboos which at the bottom were as thick as my leg. I gave up a week to felling some of them.

"While I was engaged in this work I had the worst disaster I suffered on the island. I broke the blade of my knife. I felt helpless in a hundred different ways after that. Some types of shell are sharp, but the best is no substitute for steel. With the bamboos I had cut I could construct nothing better than a sort of catamaran. It had a faggot-like float to either side, with an open framework in the middle on which I sat, dangling my legs in the water. I drove the thing along with a paddle made from a plank I found washed up in the cove.

"I loaded this crazy craft with as many rocks as it would carry and went pearl-fishing. I would slip off my perch with a rock in my arms. There were plenty of oysters on the bottom. I would grab one, or one in each hand if I could, and get to the surface as quickly as possible. It was a crude method and I nearly burst my lungs time and again. How long it took to come up! But I got a lot of pearls."

"Can you say how many?" Angus enquired.

"The number does not signify, for most of them were small. I wanted a few exceptionally fine ones. When I had collected half a dozen beauties I gave up pearling altogether."

"What was your reason for doing that?"

"I had proved that there were plenty of pearls in the lagoon. I had dived in a fixed area and harvested a certain number of pearls. By exploratory dives elsewhere I had satisfied myself that almost the whole lagoon-bottom was equally populated by oysters. But by my crude fishing methods it would have taken a lifetime to collect enough to finance the plan I dreamed of. Why waste precious years if it could be avoided? If I could get home quickly

48

I could, on the strength of my samples, raise enough to finance a properly equipped expedition which could do the necessary fishing in a fraction of the time. So all my interest and endeavour turned to getting home. I took my catamaran to pieces, transported it to the cove and relashed it with fresh creepers. I rigged a palm-frond sail on a three-legged mast. I corked my six fine pearls into a bamboo phial which I slung round my neck, and I cached the remaining smaller pearls in a hiding place. Then I was ready to go. But I knew it would be suicide to set off unless there were a ship that I could head for. There are a few small islands within some hundreds of miles of Ecalpemos. But I could scarcely hope to strike those and would be little better off if I did. The nearest mainland is over a thousand miles away. Even if my catamaran did not come to pieces I would be drowned by spray in the first rough weather.

"So I spent my days watching for a ship. From any part of the rim only a limited arc of the ocean was visible. So I climbed the mountain. It was not difficult, but it was very steep. The surface of the white deposit was hard as enamel, and slippery. Also there were the birds which did not approve at all—or else they wanted me to try my hand at flying. But on the summit there was a flat space as big as that table—the crow's nest I called it. I'd climb up and sit there morning and afternoon, swivelling slowly round on my behind, sweeping the whole horizon.

"After only a week I saw a sail. It passed by a long way off, always to windward of the island. There was no chance of intercepting it or attracting its attention. But it gave me hope.

"That hope gradually starved to death. For months

nothing more broke the circle of dazzling blue except, very occasionally, the spout of a whale. I had long before decided that the ship I had seen the sails of was probably a whaler. Nothing else except a scientific vessel could have any business in those waters. And even a whaling captain —if I remembered my authority—was not likely to put in to an island except to careen or water his ship. Ecalpemos was no dockyard, and a mighty awkward place for watering. I had no hope, but I was obstinate. I maintained my watch.

"I was on my way up the staircase one morning and scarcely above the level of the rim when I saw a ship. She was on a course which would take her past the lee side of the island. She was not running directly with the wind, but obliquely across it. She was only a few miles away— *too close*. As likely as not she would be past and away before I could get out to her. For a moment I hesitated, for it might have been wiser to stay where I was and wave, or even climb on to the summit where I would be most conspicuous. But instead I came down the mountain so fast that it was no merit of mine I did not break my neck.

"From the rim I saw the ship again. I also saw a school of whales sporting a few miles off shore. The ship was heading directly at them.

"I'd discovered a tortoise-track which led on a downhill slant to the top of the crack. It was longer than the direct line but made faster travelling than through the scrub. I raced along it, slipped down the crack and had my catamaran in the water in a matter of minutes.

"Even so I was not quick enough to see the ship from the cove. She had passed out of sight. While I was hoisting the sail it occurred to me that for a ship to head in the direction of whales did not prove she was a whaler. If she were not I could not catch up with her, and there would be no turning back. But I had to risk that. I paddled out of the cove. The wind snatched at my little sail, and away I went.

"Soon, from the crests of the swell, I caught glimpses of the ship. Thank God she was a whaler! She had come into the wind and was lowering her boats. I had not much control of my craft, but the wind would take me close to her. For a short while I was jubilant.

"Not for long. I passed within a quarter of a mile of the ship, and no one took any notice of me. I ripped down my sail and paddled for all I was worth against the wind. But I still drew away from the ship. Now and then from the crests of the swell I caught a glimpse of one or other of the boats—always going away from me. Evidently the whales had scattered and every boat the ship had was after them, with nothing to spare for a wretched castaway. I doubted if I had even been spotted. I could see nothing most of the time except the steep blue slopes of the swell and the white waves that curled over them, for I was almost as low in the water as if I had been swimming.

"I heard the ship fire a return order to her boats. She was already a long way off. I was losing in my struggle against the wind. It blew strongly against my three-legged mast. But I continued to head towards the ship, paddling with the last of my strength.

"There was a shout behind me. I glanced back to see one of the whale-boats very close. At the helmsman's shout every rower had turned to look over his shoulder—and I have never seen such a wild bunch of faces. They seemed to me fiercer than pirates.

51

"Next moment the crest of the swell passed under me and the boat was hidden. In a very few seconds it would reappear, closer still.

"I would like to tell you that I reasoned quickly. I was as helpless as a man could be, stark naked except for the bamboo phial slung round my neck. Those wild men would want to know what it contained. When they knew —what would they care for a lonely castaway? But I did not reason. I had been too long alone upon my island among the harmless beasts and birds. I acted on the same primeval instinct which makes a frightened bitch put its young into what in its desperation seems the safest place. I took the pearls out of the phial and swallowed them."

There was a sound like a sigh in the room. Ronald coughed and swallowed as if there were something still in his throat. He drank a little water and then went on.

"They were rough folk indeed. She was a Basque whaler. The officers were French, and about half the crew. But they had been cruising two years and had suffered casualties which they'd replaced with any human stuff they could find. Burned black as I was, long-haired and bearded, they took me for a savage swept out while fishing. I did not contradict. I kept quiet. But they were not interested in me except as a strong-looking hand.

"Aboard the ship they threw me some clothes, and for three days I worked with the others, getting blubber aboard and feeding the boiling try-pots. It was stinking work. But I was happy enough. My island had sunk below the horizon, its secret kept. I had recovered my pearls and stowed them away in the pockets of my oily trousers.

"The next problem was how to get home quickly—in other words to desert. For the ship's barrels were only half-full and I had no wish to spend another year or more in cruising round the world. It was six months before I got a chance. Then by good fortune we suffered such damage in a gale off the Cape that we had to put in for repairs. Not all the precautions of the captain and his officers could prevent me getting away. That is a story for another time. I made for open country and hid until the ship sailed. Then I returned to town, and sold the smallest pearl. It weighed twenty-eight grains and I got the equivalent of ninety pounds for it. I feel sure it was worth much more. But I knew nothing about the trade. I did not know whom to go to and in any case was in no position to argue.

"I bought some decent clothes and a passage home on the first ship. Three days ago I landed in Liverpool, and here I am—with these."

Ronald took from his pocket a knotted handkerchief. He untied it and poured on to the table-cover five large pearls—two spherical, one oval, one pear-shaped, and one which in shape and colour was something like a strawberry.

The company converged upon the table.

Mrs. Mackintosh raised her head. She had neither spoken nor moved throughout the long recital. Now she fixed her pale blue eyes upon her son and asked in a voice as soft as a caress, "Well, what do you want to do?"

He answered, "I am afraid I ought to organise an expedition as soon as possible and go back to fish that lake properly. There is no time to be lost."

"Naturally, dear," said the gentle voice. "I was only wondering what your plans might be."

"I will tell you, Mother—and any man who is ready to go with me," Ronald said.

3

There was little sleep in the house of widow Mackintosh that night. No one who had listened to Ronald's story wanted to go before hearing his plans for colonising the island. They did not all commit themselves. That would not have been in the Highland character. But Ronald knew that if they were not genuinely interested they would have gone to their beds. If they saw the scheme was practical they would, after what he had said earlier, take it for granted that they could join the expedition, bringing their whole families. Since all the families of Corron were inter-related that would mean a major migration.

One man said, "To take everyone to this island of yours would cost thousands and thousands and thousands of pounds. If we had a quarter of the money we could stay at home and have porridge and bacon and eggs every morning and a dram every evening of our lives."

Ronald explained that he had never hoped or intended to take the whole party of colonists at once. His plan was in two phases, the first of which would be a raid to raise the necessary funds.

"A cattle raid?"

"No, a pearl raid."

Ronald got his first laugh—one with excitement in it.

He went on quickly to explain that he believed there was in the lagoon of Ecalpemos an ample wealth of pearls to pay for the whole migration. He proposed to go and get it with a small and carefully selected party in a sturdy little ship.

He turned to the brother who had always backed him up as a boy.

"What do you think, Sandy?"

"The first thing that worries me is the sturdy little ship," said Sandy Mackintosh.

"The ship! Don't you see what is in my mind?"

"There is a Loch Corron cutter in your mind. But it is nowhere else."

"I know yours is sold. You told me."

"They all went, Ron, when the fishing failed."

"There is the one building in the yard."

"She's building muckle slow, in spare time—just as a bit of money comes in, which is not often, or some timber."

"How much would it cost to finish her quickly?"

"A tidy lot."

"But how much?"

Every man in the room sat silent. Sandy said cautiously, "Your estimate is as good as mine. It's not just the cutter—there would be stores and equipment needed too, I'm thinking. These five pearls you've brought back would never pay for all that, surely."

"Not the half of it. But I can use them as bait. Leave the money side to me. Now then, what do you think of this raid?"

Every man in the room had handled a Loch Corron cutter from childhood until the bad days came, and so felt that his opinion was worth giving. There was plenty of

55

talking after that, plenty of different suggestions. But it was generally agreed that a Loch Corron cutter crewed by Corron men could sail any ocean of the world and cover twelve thousand miles in something like six months.

"Good," said Ronald. "That's what I thought myself. Now what about the men?"

"Sandy should be skipper," Bruce said. "There's none better. And you can see he is hitching his breeks to go— if his wife will let him. I don't mind coming as mate myself and navigating you to this island if you will just tell me the longitude and latitude."

"I will do that," Ronald said, smiling. He could see that the old sailor was as excited as a boy although he tried to hide it. "How many will we need for crew?"

"Three or four besides Sandy and me—eh, Sandy? All the young men will be tumbling over each other to come. But three or four will do if we must keep the numbers down."

This, after discussion, was agreed. But a man said:

"We'll give you the sailors, all right. But how do you get the pearls? There are mighty few of us who can swim."

"I have seen native pearl-divers," Bruce said reminiscently. "It's a wonderful sight. They can go down to fifteen fathoms. Some say to twenty, but I doubt that's an exaggeration."

"I don't want natives on my cutter," Sandy said.

"Nor on the island—if we can help it," said Ronald. "My plan is to be self-contained if possible from the start to finish. We must take a land party besides the crew."

He explained that since there was no anchorage the

56

cutter would not be able to remain safely at the island for any length of time. Therefore it would be best for her to drop a land party and go straight on to the nearest port for a refit, which in any case would be necessary. Meanwhile the land party would fish as best they could. When the cutter returned—say between two and four months later—it was to be hoped that the land party, of which he would be in charge, would have collected enough pearls.

"But how?" he was asked.

"I can dive a bit. And it may be possible to dredge. I will find out about dredging. You must leave that to me."

"We have trust in you, Ronald," a man said. "But just suppose you don't succeed."

"Then Sandy will have to go off again and recruit half a dozen native divers whether he likes it or not. But I trust that won't be necessary. It would make the raid much longer and more expensive."

There was a moment of silence. Then Ronald went on energetically:

"You will have quite enough to bother about building the cutter. Use all you have on that—and all the credit you can raise. Leave everything else to me."

On this note the discussion ended. The people dispersed. Ronald followed them outside, saying good nights.

It was still raining. But no one minded that.

4

Ronald faced Mr. Joseph Kalman across a table covered with black velvet. Kalman's private office was ornate and he himself was over-dressed. But his face was the face of a mystic, tight-drawn and pale as old parchment, with dark and shining eyes.

"Let me see them, Mr. Mackintosh, let me see them," he said impatiently and with a slight lisp.

Ronald placed his five pearls on the black velvet.

Mr. Kalman drew in his breath between his teeth and leaned forward in his chair until his nose was close above the gems.

"Very interesting," he said. "I am always happy to see pearls. Where do they come from?"

"It so happens——" Ronald began.

"Do not tell me, Mr. Mackintosh. I will tell you."

Mr. Kalman took a lens from his pocket and examined each pearl long and carefully. He picked them up between finger and thumb, turned them on the palm of his hand. He peered from every angle, as if trying to see inside them. He grunted.

"I said I was interested. Now I am. Mr. Mackintosh, I *shall* tell you where these pearls come from. I always can do that. But let us do it this time the other way round, eh? I will tell you first the places that they do not come from . . . Not the Persian Gulf, that's sure. They have not the lustre . . . Not Madras or Ceylon . . . Not China. They have not what I call to myself the fresh-water look."

At each statement he glanced up at Ronald with a quick, decisive shake of the head.

"Australia? I do not think—no, definitely. The texture is a little like—but no. Not white and more lustre . . . No parti-colour—not from Panama . . . Not Venezuela . . . Not California . . . Let us cross the ocean

58

again. Not Celebes or Timor Sea—too fine . . . Then mid-ocean. But they can't be from Tahiti with that colour . . . Mr. Mackintosh, where the blazes do these pearls come from?"

Ronald evaded the question by asking another.

"You really can tell as a rule, sir, the area where a pearl has been fished?"

"The area—I can tell within a hundred miles."

"What an extraordinary gift!"

"It is not more extraordinary than that of a wine connoisseur, Mr. Mackintosh. I taste with my eyes. I have been doing that for fifty-five years. These pearls of yours have a flavour which I do not know. Perhaps others would not detect it. I do. They are from the Pacific. That is certain. But the Pacific is a very large ocean."

"What would you be prepared to offer for them?" Ronald asked.

Mr. Kalman became once more absorbed in the pearls. He studied them again, and weighed them. He made a calculation on paper. At last he said in a tone of finality, "Three hundred and fifty pounds."

"They are worth double that," Ronald said.

"To you, Mr. Mackintosh—very likely. But not to me. I have to sell what I buy. This strawberry. It is very strange, very amusing. But my clients are serious. The strawberry is worth nothing to me. Of the others, two are of poor shape. The remaining two are beauties. They might be included in a queen's necklace. But with what other pearls could I match them? With cousins, perhaps, but not sisters. My necklaces must be strings of sisters."

"I could bring you a hundred, two hundred sister pearls

if you would invest in an expedition to collect them," Ronald said.

"Your suggestion is most original, Mr. Mackintosh. But—I have buyers all over the world. They trade with the pearlers. They do not subsidise the pearlers. It would not be possible to exercise control."

"Would you not take the risk for a rich and untapped area?" Ronald asked.

"All my life I have been taking risks. But only when there was no other way. May I give you a piece of advice? Never try to sell anything unless you know at least as much about the business as the person to whom you try to sell. I do not believe that you know much about the pearl-trade. Therefore, as a pearl-trader, I cannot feel confidence in your proposition. You must go somewhere else, to someone who is ready to take more risk than I am."

"Who would do that?"

The merchant shrugged his shoulders and said good day.

Joseph Kalman was not the first pearl merchant whom Ronald had visited. Since coming to London from Loch Corron he had been to a dozen or more. They had all made offers for his pearls, several better than Kalman's. But the figure never approached the amount needed even for the raid.

As he walked back towards his lodgings he had noticed in a bookshop window a volume entitled *The Voyage of the Swan*. It was by Captain Matthews. The bookseller told Ronald that it had only recently been published, but already had sold well. Captain Matthews had been praised by the critics for his bluff and readable style. "A regular old sea-dog—doesn't mince his words," the bookseller said, laughing.

Ronald continued thoughtfully upon his way. Undoubtedly potential backers would take him more seriously if they knew he had served on the *Swan*. But before parting with any money they would refer to Captain Matthews. Then the secret of the island would be out for anyone who cared to profit from it while he, Ronald, as likely as not was being detained as a deserter.

'I would rather reef a topsail in a gale than have to raise money,' he thought.

He longed for a friend who could advise and help him. He could express himself frankly and openly to a friend, and a friend would need no guarantee. But the only ones rich enough to help him dated from Oxford days ten years before. Of those it seemed to him the likeliest was John Warden, who had wanted to go to sea with him and at whose home he had once stayed as a guest. He wrote to Warden Hall in Wiltshire, and received a pressing invitation to go down.

His friend's father had died and he had become Sir John, very much the lord of the manor. He was married, with four children. He was a Justice of the Peace and master of foxhounds. He greeted Ronald with great warmth and *bonhomie*.

"This is the best of good fortune! The dear old rolling stone turned up again!"

"He hopes to gather some moss," said Ronald, and told the story of his island.

Sir John listened with the greatest interest. At the end he burst out, "My dear Ronald, why did you not tell me this story eight or nine years ago?"

"Because it had not happened then!"

"Then I would not only have backed you with all I had.

61

I would have gone with you. Now—I have nothing to give."

They were walking through the park. On their left the west wing of the hall glowed red and gold in the evening sun. Ronald looked at his friend.

"You think I exaggerate, Ronald. But it is so. In the old days I had only a modest allowance, but it was mine. Now I have more duties and responsibilities than money to meet them. I do not even feel that my time is my own. The estate has inherited me."

Ronald changed the subject and hid his disappointment.

In the drawing-room that evening John Warden mentioned his friend's 'desert island' to his wife. She asked Ronald to tell her his adventures. He did so while she listened, her head bowed over her embroidery. She enquired about the island itself. He described it.

At the end she said to her husband, "It sounds just the place for Harry."

That was all. But next day Mary Warden, in the presence of her husband, told Ronald that she had a little money of her own and that she would like, subject to one condition, to invest a thousand pounds in the island venture. Mary's business approach would scarcely have impressed Mr. Joseph Kalman, but she knew very clearly what she wanted. She wanted Ronald to take her brother Harry Bentley with him. As for the money, if Ronald could later return it she would be pleased. If by way of interest he could add a pearl necklace she would be delighted. But what mattered was that he should take Harry with him and look after him well.

Having said this she smiled sweetly at Ronald and left him to think over her proposition.

Directly she had left the room Ronald turned to John.

"What——" He checked himself and began again. "What is Harry Bentley's particular interest?" he asked.

"At the moment, a most unsuitable lady," John said, smiling. "Harry is a worry to his sister. But he is a charming fellow. Let me see—seven years younger than we are. He did everything at Oxford except pass examinations. He was popular with everyone except the university authorities."

"Please be serious," Ronald said.

"One can't be about Harry. But he has not one real vice, I promise you. He only suffers from too much energy and a Why-shouldn't-I? point of view on life. You will like him and find him useful. He is a poet at heart and a first-class athlete. He'll dive for pearls for you, I am sure. He is a mountaineer, rides well——"

"All this and a thousand pounds?" Ronald said.

"There is no catch. I will be absolutely frank with you. Mary thinks—and I agree with her—that it would be the making of Harry if he travelled widely with a responsible and strong-minded person like yourself, and had a hard adventurous life for the next year or two. Have a talk with him. I am sure you will like him. I will arrange for him to meet you in London."

Before returning to London, Ronald went to Oxford. He hoped to trace two or three other friends of undergraduate days who might help him without insisting that he should become shepherd of their black sheep.

The head porter of his college recognised him immediately—which raised his spirits to an illogical degree. They

63

had a long chat about old times in the cosy little room above the gate. Ronald told as little as he politely could about himself. He sought to draw the porter out, to glean useful information from his encyclopædic store of human knowledge. The result was not encouraging. One friend had gone bankrupt, another was in Canada, a third was dead.

Ronald went out into the quad and stood there, surrounded by the grey walls from which he had run away ten years before. What had he gained by following the road which he had chosen? Nothing, unless he managed quickly to launch his expedition. At Corron the ship-building was held up. But they trusted in his ability to raise the money. His own people rated him high. They did not think of him as someone who had dropped out of life, a deserter believed drowned.

He walked away from the college. Young men, eager, confident, laughing, brushed past him in the street. He escaped into an alley between tall buildings. For a moment he was alone. Then from around a corner there came rapidly towards him an imposing figure, white hair flying, gown billowing, arms full of books.

"Professor Browning," Ronald exclaimed involuntarily.

The big man halted, peered and nodded, "Good day. Excuse me, I have not a hand. How nice to see you. How are you getting on?"

"I'm Mackintosh," said Ronald, who had decided to take a chance.

"Of course I know your name," the Professor said crossly. "Never forget my pupils. But it is difficult to keep up with them. They move on so fast. Let me see, where——"

64

"The *Swan*," Ronald said.

There was a moment of silent scrutiny, then an explosion. "Ronald Mackintosh, the scholar-sailor! My dear fellow, we all thought you were dead. Come to my rooms. I must hear all about it."

Ronald told his story without reserve, only asking that it should be treated as confidential. "Naturally, naturally," Browning said, but his interest was of another sort. He asked a hundred scientific questions which Ronald did his best to answer. The clocks of Oxford struck the quarters and the hours. Half the night passed unnoticed.

"My dear fellow, a scientific party must go there as soon as possible, adequately supported, properly equipped."

"I am impatient to go back myself, sir," Ronald answered. "But I am held up for want of the necessary funds."

"That cannot be a serious difficulty. A public appeal in the name of science—I believe the Royal Society itself would support it."

Ronald said, "Do you not think, sir, that a small private expedition would serve better? It could be arranged more simply and quickly, and time is so important. The island as you know has not been claimed by any country. On the charts it is merely a danger to navigation. Any rumour of its true value would cause a rush of claimants, perhaps nationally supported. A public appeal over the signature of the Royal Society would be internationally discussed. And then——"

"If that is a risk, it must be accepted," Browning said. "The secret of that island is how it appeared in mid-ocean, how it has been populated with the plants and animals you describe. What I propose is a scientific

65

expedition to answer these questions. Science cannot be kept secret. It is the birthright of the whole world."

He paused to light his pipe. Ronald sat looking at his imposing bulk. Then, speaking in quick, urgent sentences, he launched on a description of how his own people in Corron were struggling to live. He told of his dreams for their good which had started on the island. He sketched the two-phase plan—the quick, concentrated pearling venture, then a migration of men, women and children with domestic animals, seeds, agricultural instruments, tools.

"You might consider *that* as a scientific experiment of great value to humanity. I remember hearing you on board the *Swan* discussing why people of hot countries tend to be lazy. Is climate the cause, or something inherent in the race? Well, sir, take a party of Scotsmen and Scotswomen—industrious, intelligent, good farmers and fishermen, skilled shipwrights and artisans, the women clever spinners and weavers—what would they make of a place which rewarded their efforts?"

The professor smiled. "An experiment in the grand manner! Well, you risked your life for that island. I did not. You have the right to do things in your own way."

"I only wish I could," said Ronald, and described his misadventures with the London merchants.

"Have you tried Pinkerton and Powell?" Browning asked.

"No. Are they in the pearl trade?"

"That is one of their interests. They have many others. It is a widespread organisation—world-wide."

"What will they think of me with my five pearls? I have found that the bigger the firm, the less they like

66

dealing with a single individual who is not even connected with the trade."

"I have known George Pinkerton for many years," Browning said thoughtfully. "His agents send me marine specimens every now and then, things they don't know about. It is an arrangement to our mutual advantage. I believe that if I gave you a letter to Pinkerton he would be ready to deal with you."

"That really is kind of you," Ronald said, deeply moved.

"It is the best I can do, Mackintosh. We monks of science have no money for the calcareous concretions you are so interested in. But people are beginning to respect us."

Professor Browning's letter—whatever he said in it— had a surprising effect. Ronald was more than a little mystified by the result. Mr. Pinkerton saw him directly he presented himself. He admired the pearls, but made no offer for them. He gave the impression that so small a number was of no interest to his firm. He also appeared sceptical of the existence of a pearling area which he did not already know of.

"Where is this island?" he asked point-blank.

When Ronald hesitated, Pinkerton became red in the face and said that he trusted a man whom Professor Browning recommended and that he expected to be trusted in return. How else could they talk business?

Ronald told him the position of the island and its name on the chart.

Pinkerton sat squashing his large soft face into strange shapes. Ronald watched him fascinated. Pinkerton's face resumed its normal form, and he said, "If you will come back at twelve o'clock tomorrow, Mr. Mackintosh, I will tell you whether we can help you or not."

Ronald arrived punctually next day—to be asked to wait because the senior partner was engaged. As he sat impatiently in the waiting-room a young man came in and talked to him. He was pleasant and polite. He had some knowledge of the East, from which he had returned three months ago. Ronald found him good company and had quite forgotten his impatience when he was at last invited to go into Pinkerton's office.

"I have decided to offer you an advance of one thousand five hundred pounds towards financing your expedition," Pinkerton said without preamble.

Ronald started and stared.

"You on your side," Pinkerton went on, "will repay this advance in the form of pearls and also give us first refusal of all pearls obtained. Furthermore you will include in your party a man nominated by me."

"It will be a very small party——" Ronald began.

"You doubt if he will fit in? I assure you he will. He happens to know a lot about pearls and pearling. It would not be in my own interest to give you anyone but a first-class man. I will introduce you to him."

A few minutes later Ronald was shaking hands with the young man who had kept him company in the waiting-room. He was introduced as Geoffrey Partridge.

Ronald was so relieved at being offered more than half the money he required on such light conditions—particularly since Pinkerton did not demand any share in exploring the island, only a first offer of the pearls—that he accepted gratefully on the spot.

When he returned to his lodgings the landlady told him

68

that a Mr. Bentley had been waiting for him for the last hour and more. He was a friend, was he not? She had showed the gentleman into the sitting-room. She hoped that was all right.

Ronald said that it was quite all right. He climbed the three floors to his rooms, thinking that it was too good to be true. Almost certainly Harry Bentley would prove impossible at any price. But if it seemed possible to fit him in—then, after weeks of disappointment, all the money necessary for the raid would have been made available in a single day.

He opened his door. There was no one in the sitting-room. The adjoining bedroom, little more than a cubicle, was empty too. Harry Bentley had evidently become bored with waiting and gone away.

Ronald sat down at the desk. As he did so he saw out of the corner of his eye a figure at one of the windows, a hundred feet above road level. A man climbed into the room. He was well dressed, but his face suggested a prize-fighter—notched nose, a front tooth with its tip chipped off obliquely, eyes which although they certainly did not squint (they were particularly direct) were unusual and unmatched in colour or light.

"Mr. Mackintosh? I'm Harry Bentley," he said angrily. "Why do things happen like this? I've been sitting in that chair for an hour twiddling my thumbs like a curate. Every now and then I looked out of the window to see if anyone was coming into the house. Of course I noticed that ledge and began to wonder if it was possible to traverse from one window to the other. At last I had to try it—just as you were coming in. You must think me horribly rude."

"No," Ronald said, "I didn't think that."

"How nice of you! Mary—you know my sister?—told me you have got an island where there is a great mountain smoking with birds, fantastic vegetation, and Kubla Khan caves. She said you might take me there, and let me loose among all those south sea atolls."

In Harry's ugly, essentially masculine face, Ronald suddenly had a glimpse of Mary Warden's fairy beauty.

"I am going there to live very simply and to work very hard, fishing for pearl oysters. Do you think you could do that?" he asked.

"I've eaten plenty of oysters. It can't be difficult to fish them. They pull them up by the ton."

"These are a different sort of oysters. These are as big as soup plates. I don't think one could fish them in the same way as in England."

"Why not?"

"I don't know exactly. I've been told one can't. But I have got to make certain about that."

"Then let us go down to Whitstable and find out."

By the time they reached Whitstable it was evening and it was drizzling. The mud, the Thames Estuary and the sky were grey. The little town was grey, with damp streets, nobody about. It seemed doubtful whether they would learn much about oyster-fishing. But Ronald had agreed to the journey largely for the opportunity it offered of getting to know Harry Bentley.

Together they walked round the harbour where the fishing boats were dozing together, their bows against the quay.

The place was deserted except for one young fellow who sat with his back against a shed, busy at some fisherman's task. In the general greyness he was remarkable for his colour. He had a round red face and carrot hair.

Harry strode up to him and said good evening.

"My friend and I want to find out how to fish oysters. Can you tell us?"

"Dredge 'em," said the carrot-haired youth.

"Yes, I thought so. But what is a dredge like?"

"There's three here," said the fisherman. He indicated the complex of wood, wire, cordage, metal and netting which was spread about him. He went on, "You can't see so well 'cause I've taken 'em to pieces like. Greasin' and mendin'. But—surely you know what a dredge is."

"I think I can make it out," Ronald said. "A sort of big, heavy shrimping-net you tow behind a boat."

"I suppose you might say it's like that. But I don't see why you got to bring up shrimps."

"At what angle do you tow it?" Ronald went on. "I mean, is it weighted to ride upright, or to dredge almost horizontally?"

"That's all according."

"To what?"

"Speed, depth, bottom."

"Could we see one being used?"

"In May? You'll have to wait till the end of August, mister."

"You couldn't just show me how it works?"

"Well—the gear's all stowed away."

Harry asked, "Would your trawl fish up oysters as large as soup plates?"

"Show it the oysters and it would fish 'em," the other said, grinning with disbelief.

71

"They are that size, and with pearls in them," Harry went on. "It's a desert island——"

"A desert island!"

The fisherman rose to his feet. He was short, round, far from handsome. But his face was alight.

"A desert island! That's the only book I could ever read. Parrots and treasure and dancing girls in grass skirts——"

"I'm afraid there are no dancing girls," said Harry, laughing.

"Must be, mister. Always are. I could show you in print."

He turned to Ronald. "If all you want is just to see how a dredge works—well, come down any day next week and I'll take you out. If you don't see me, ask for Red Mallett."

"Red Mullet?" said Harry, still laughing.

"No-o! That's so stale it stinks. Mallett—what you hit blokes over the head with."

5

With money in the bank, Ronald pressed forward his preparations. He began buying stores. He sent a draft to Corron, and was assured that the building of the cutter was progressing at full speed. They were working all day, and at night by torchlight, he was told. His brother wrote that he had three excellent young boys for crew, but he was anxious about the land party, for to recruit for that as well would rob the village of the best of its youth.

Ronald was little concerned by this since he already had two men for the land party. Harry Bentley was tireless and stimulating, and he liked him. He would have taken him even without Lady Warden's thousand pounds investment. In a different way he also liked Geoffrey Partridge. Partridge was a quieter, less energetic character, but seemed more trustworthy. Ronald had several discussions with him about which method of fishing was to be used. Partridge had only seen pearls brought up by divers, either naked or with apparatus. He had no experience of dredging. In fact the only form of pearl-oyster dredge mentioned in the firm's records was that used by the primitive natives of the Sulu Sea. It was a sort of heavily weighted rake, one prong of which might occasionally enter the open shell of an oyster and be gripped as the mollusc attempted to close. Nothing could sound more inefficient.

Yet Ronald had firmly set his face against taking divers. Apart from other considerations there would be no room for them on the cutter. He said he felt sure that a Thames Estuary dredge would be suitable for the lagoon if only he could be certain of being able to use it to the best advantage. He had gone back to Whitstable for the promised demonstration. It had not been as instructive as it might have been, however, for outside the fishing season it had been impossible to fish the oyster-beds. Also Red Mallett, although clearly an expert in every aspect of his trade, was quite incapable of explaining how anything should be done. "Well, you just do it, if you see what I mean," was a typical phrase.

"I know," said Harry during a discussion at his club. "Let's take him with us. Why not? Otherwise we will spend our time fiddling with that horrible gear and arguing how to use it. I want to enjoy myself."

"It's an excellent idea," said Ronald. "But he would never come. He told me that he had only once been out of Kent—when he was blown over to the Essex side of the Estuary."

"I'll get him if you say the word," said Harry.

"By all means have a try!"

Harry succeeded. He made some private financial arrangement with Mallett. (He was free with his money and credit.) He also, it was hinted, made certain promises among which was included a round trip of the South Sea Islands when the work was done. At any rate, Red Mallett became the fourth member of the land party.

Ronald left his three English recruits to collect the stores, and went up to Scotland.

He arrived just in time for the launching—by his mother, in the presence of every man and woman and child in the village. Old Mrs. Mackintosh, a bent but independent figure, walked slowly to the cutter where it stood upon the stocks. She tapped the bows with her stick and said:

"I name you *Loch Corron*. God bless you and those you carry. You will never be out of the thoughts of those who wait at home."

Then she stepped back a few paces. The hammers rang. The cutter ran joyfully into the sea.

Three weeks later she sailed. Her skipper, Sandy Mackintosh, left a wife and two children behind him. Old Bruce, the mate, was a childless widower. The other three were young and unmarried, little more than boys. Willie and Johnnie were brothers, but as different as night from day. Willie was big, dark, well-meaning and slow. Johnny was slim, quick-witted, very fair, with the face of an angel —and the heart of a demon, some said. The other common seaman was Dean—tall, thin, spectacled and serious.

These five men, Ronald, and the three Englishmen who were picked up with the stores in the Port of London, were the ship's whole company. Nor could she, without considerable discomfort, have carried any more. But on the run down the Irish Sea and up the Channel she had proved herself a good sea boat, and all had confidence in her.

From London in June the *Loch Corron* sailed for the other side of the world.

Chapter Four

I

The only thing which had changed was the sky.

A single-masted vessel sailing steadily over the huge un-
dulations of the ocean swell yet seeming to get nowhere
because there was nothing by which progress could be
judged—nothing but moving waves and the paling stars
of dawn. Two men on deck, one drowsing with folded
arms and chin on chest, the other at the helm—Harry
Bentley, who thought these thoughts. Seven men below,
two dressed and ready to come up at a call, the others in
their bunks no doubt, unless one of them was already preparing the morning brew. The individual occupations had
interchanged continually, but the pattern was the same.
Not much difference between night and day—far less
than on land. Rough weather meant less sleep, fair
weather making good—of cordage, canvas, hours of rest.
Nothing in sight but sky and restless water.

It had been the same for nearly half a year. The little
ship, her people, the indifferent sea. True they had
occasionally watched another ship passing like a slow
gesture of indifference. They had glimpsed the living
things of the ocean—which took no notice of them. And
three times they had called in for water and fresh food.
But those glimpses, and these brief, busy interruptions had

only accentuated their own microcosmic loneliness and the routine which ruled their lives. They had never had time to feel again their kinship with the land. Quite the reverse. Harry remembered the first call, at Tenerife. It had followed a week of—in his view then—the roughest weather possible. Approaching the quay he, as the most athletic, had been ordered to the bow. When they came close enough he leaped ashore with a rope and ran to a bollard to make fast. That was what he intended. In fact he staggered about, bereft of balance. The stone quay seemed to pitch and roll. He had found his sea-legs at the expense of becoming estranged to the land. They took what they needed from the land and within twenty-four hours were out of sight of it again.

The little ship, the sea and the sky. The sky had changed. It was not the soft-textured English sky. By day it had become metal-hard and the sun went almost straight up and down it. By night it was still more altered, for the stars had changed. Harry could feel no sense of community with these strangers, as he had nothing in common with this southern ocean which seemed as vast as the sky. Strange land, yes, he would welcome that. Land you could come to know—explore, walk over, enjoy at ease. His bursting energy longed to express itself on land, not in a monotonous struggle against amorphous water under stranger stars.

A glimmer raced over the ocean. Harry saw the fiery topknot of the sun. It stretched its arms along the eastern horizon and in no time it would heave itself right up.

But something broke the straight line of the horizon— something shining, with strong outlines, not many miles away.

"Land!" Harry shouted with all the force of pent-up feelings.

The dozing man woke like an echo. From below came rumblings of activity. Ronald was the first to come up and identify his island. In a very short time everybody was on deck in various stages of dress—a hairy, unkempt, grinning company. They held to shrouds or the mast, silently gazing. Bruce, by far the oldest, was the exception. He balanced sturdily, without support, and expounded at length on the virtues of the sea-dog's method which had got them where they were. He had not set a straight course, not he. If you did that and missed you did not know which side you were. To hell with unreliable chronometers and complicated mathematics! The noon sun gave you your latitude and no mistakes possible. So he had aimed 'a safe distance' to the westward. Having reached the island's latitude he had re-set the course due eastward—"sure as if I could see the line in the water", and here they were! They had even made the landfall half a day earlier than calculated!

Skipper Sandy—a more conventional navigator, but tactful—encouraged the flow of self-congratulation. Ronald, his eyes fixed on his island, said nothing at all. Suddenly he called out and pointed. A white tern came darting to the ship and hung above the deck, examining each man with its soft and thoughtful eye.

The cook of the day remembered the kettle and hurried to the galley. A few minutes later a hand came up through the forward hatch, holding a steaming cup. This was at once taken. Another and another followed until everybody who stood swaying to the movements of the deck had a mug in one hand. They sipped and began

78

talking about the island which they could see in detail now that the light was full. It was grim as a fortress. The breakers which bombarded it were not yet audible, but the white explosions leaped half-way up the cliffs and hung thinning in the air until the next salvo came.

"Good thing the night weren't an hour longer," Red Mallett said to Geoffrey Partridge.

Throughout the long voyage they had worked as a team. Not only the common tasks but spontaneous friendship had bound Corron men and 'foreigners' into a unit. But within ten minutes of sighting the island the land party and the ship's crew proper were talking in separate groups. It seemed natural when the skipper took over the helm and began giving orders only to the Corron men, while Ronald led his three below.

They already knew the disembarkation plan, but he ran through it again when they had packed up the last of their belongings and were eating breakfast.

"Will the weather be good enough for landing, Ronald?" Geoffrey asked. Being the least strong physically and the most imaginative he was a little nervous.

"I would prefer it calmer. But I think it will do—although we won't know for certain until we reach Instep Bay. Come on deck if you have finished."

They were racing along under the overhanging cliffs of the Heel. The closeness gave a sense of extraordinary speed. And the rocks were frightening. Waves licked up them, and spat. Spray spotted the sun-baked deck. Here and there the water span in angry vortices with hissing foam. But the big noise was hollow, hungry. The Corron men had grown used to it already. They were accustomed from childhood to deep water under high cliffs. But perhaps they were showing off just a little to the others who had suddenly become landsmen again. At any rate, apart from the skipper at the helm, they had their backs to the rocks. They were unlashing the flat-bottomed boat and a big roll of netting, timber, iron and cordage—the dismantled dredges.

The land party, having stowed their kit against the gunwale or wherever it was safe and handy, had nothing to do but look at the island. They only saw the concave face of the cliff and the steeply sloping forehead of bare rock ending in a line of scrub bushes which stood up *en brosse* against the sky. The ship was so close in that the men could not appreciate the shape of the coastline, until they reached a wide bay which, somewhat short of the half-way line, indented the shoe-shaped island. Then the *Loch Corron*, holding her course, began to trend away from the shore. The mountain came into view, looking very tall at that steep angle, and with a haze of birds swinging about it. Ronald, who had gone to join his brother at the helm, indicated a point at the head of the bay, close to where one of the basalt buttresses was rooted in the cliff.

"The cove," he said.

They all looked at it. At that distance it showed only as an upsurge of fighting waves. They had been told that calm water was behind this barrier. But at best it could only be a very small cove.

The skipper continued a little longer on his course, then went about and ran in towards the cove, close hauled. The cutter nosed her way forward delicately, with shivering sails.

A hundred yards from the cove's mouth Sandy set her a-back and she lay heaving on the cross seas. The waves near the head of the bay moved in two directions—with the wind and in opposition—a large-scale eddy. The two lines of waves, growing in height as the bay constricted them, closed on the cove with a scissor action. Where they met they tumbled over each other, frothing, and seemed to run into the cove where they broke up in spurts and fountains.

The cutter's own boat, a steady craft, was put into the water and manned by four rowers and a helmsman, Bruce. She took only a light load for the first attempt. Ronald stood up in the bow. When the rowers started, pulling as hard as if they were in a race, he gave directions to the helmsman by extending one arm or the other, and shouted to the oars to slow or to increase their pace. The boat travelled in the middle line between the V of the waves. It swerved to starboard to avoid rough water, then raced at full-speed along the crest of tumbling foam and through the entrance. The entrance was no wider than a gateway. Beyond it the rowers thrust against their oars, back-watering, for the cove itself was scarcely twenty paces across. It was roughly circular, with smooth rock sides and shingle at the further end, reminiscent of a river pool below a fall. The water was calm but gyrating. It tended to turn the boat directly she lost speed. Ronald vaulted out and, waist deep, pulled the bow on to the shingle. It had been an exciting, but comparatively simple, operation.

They unloaded, left Geoffrey who had been one of the oarsmen, and started back for the cutter. The return was quite easy. With each stroke beyond the entrance of the cove they had more room to manœuvre, and the waves being less and less constricted were less high. But Geoffrey watched the boat with anxiety. It occurred to him that

81

if there were an accident he might remain a lonely castaway with a minimum of stores. His first impression of the island had not been favourable. It was a hard, unfriendly place.

With the second trip the flat-bottomed dinghy was taken in tow. It danced like a kite behind a running child. Ronald guided the cutter's boat safely through the complex of uneasy waters. But the dinghy got caught between two clapping waves. It was thrown into the air, came down on its side and was half filled with water. But the cutter's boat was already through the entrance. They reached the shore safely.

This time Harry was left. He helped to heave the dinghy above the tide line and to pile the batch of stores. Then he went exploring. Geoffrey remained where he was and watched the boat, moving his hand as if he himself were steering. She shipped a wave which rocked her and put the rowers off their stroke. Geoffrey's imagination flew back to disaster—to being left alone on the island with Harry. He realised that this was silly. He allowed the thought to remain as a joke against himself. But partly he was serious, for he was in a highly-strung state at this critical phase of the venture. What would Harry be like? He found it difficult to make up his mind. Before starting from England he had supposed he would get to know his shipmates inside out. That had not proved the case. He knew their appetites, their capacity for sleep and a number of very personal and unimportant details one would never discover in ordinary life. As far as character went he knew their reactions in a crowded uncomfortable place, how quick they were to go aloft or on deck in bad weather, and he knew their seaman's capabilities. But especially with those in the other watch—as Harry had been—he had scarcely talked on general subjects or discovered how much he had in common outside the voyage and its purpose. He had sometimes been surprised at his own behaviour, cramped, in mid-ocean. People acted very differently on shore. What sort of a companion would Harry be? By the way he was scrambling about the slabs he would soon be a dead one.

"For God's sake be careful," Geoffrey shouted.

"This is heaven!" Harry's enthusiastic voice came back.

Meanwhile the boat had reached the cutter. There remained the dredges and too many other stores to make one safe load.

"Never mind," Sandy said. "I'm going ashore as passenger to have a peep at this island of yours. Red, you can wait with your dredges. Keep the helm, Bruce."

Bruce, under the eye of his skipper, took the boat in faultlessly.

While she was unloading, Sandy, Ronald and the mate climbed to the rim.

"You can't do more than glimpse the lagoon through the trees," Ronald said.

"That's all you did before you decided to stay that first time," said Sandy, an arm on his brother's shoulder. "It's enough for me too. You chose a fine spot."

They descended to the shore and the skipper returned to his ship.

On her final trip the boat travelled well in spite of the dredges which cramped the efforts of the rowers. She dodged an explosion of water and swung to port, straight for the entrance, then less than three lengths away. Next moment a chance waterspout gave an uppercut to the projecting dredge and tipped the boat. Ronald was almost thrown overboard and in recovering his balance rocked the boat still more. One of the rowers caught a crab, going over backwards on to the man behind him. The boat slewed to the current. She would have struck a side of the entrance if another of the rowers had not warded off the collision with an oar. But she had lost way and wallowed. A pack of waves leaped aboard. In no time she was so full that she began to flood at every movement. Bruce remained seated in the water, bellowing orders. The rowers splashed about ineffectively. Ronald grabbed the end of the painter and plunged overboard. He swam, found his feet and waded. Geoffrey, and Harry a moment later, rushed in to help him. The rowers stood up and punted. They got the bow on to the shingle.

Red Mallett scrambled out and shook himself like a wet dog. He looked round with a serene expression on his ugly face and said, "Turned out nice after all."

They laughed or cursed him. The silly joke gave a vent for their feelings. Then they unloaded the stores. Everything was soaked, of course, including the firearms.

"Open one of the cans of lamp oil," Ronald said. "We must get these weapons washed out and dried at once."

Dripping themselves, they sat down to the task, bathing the working parts in paraffin.

Bruce asked, "Will I go back for the guns we have on board?"

"No, no. You may need them—more likely than we. And these will work fine in any case. But you go back. I can read Sandy's expression from here."

After a very little more conversation they shook hands all round and parted.

"See you on the first of April."

"We'll be back."

"All sacks and boxes full of pearls."

"Behave yourselves. Look after the cutter and leave the women alone."

"Remember that letter to my father."

They waved. The boat was heading out through the entrance. She weathered the broken water. Then some of the rowers waved back. One of them shouted something and a laugh followed the indistinguishable words.

"Think of when we see them coming back!" said Geoffrey.

"Plenty to do before then," Ronald said.

Red murmured, "Three months of oystering before I goes home and starts oystering again."

The four men remained standing close together, watching the boat. They saw it come alongside the cutter. ("Watch the paint!" Harry said, imitating the skipper.) They saw the crew go aboard, the boat hoisted. They could still distinguish everybody—the squat figure of Bruce, the young giant Willie, little fair Johnnie, the spare and slightly stooping Dean. They were hurrying to obey an order from Sandy at the helm. The four men ashore knew exactly what they were doing. They could feel the ropes, the changing movements of the little ship.

The cutter nosed up into the wind, close hauled, and headed back toward the west. She glided out of sight behind the rocks of the cove, the men about her deck too busy to look at those ashore.

Somehow there was more of a sense of parting than when they had left home.

2

They were finishing the reassembling of the weapons when there burst out a noise startlingly loud and strange —a gargantuan gasping and throat clearing.

"One of the blow-holes I told you about," said Ronald, intent upon a trigger mechanism.

Harry jumped to his feet.

"It was quite close. I must find the cave."

"When we have finished this job we must start carrying the stores to the lagoon," said Ronald, still without looking up.

Harry looked down at him with exasperation. Then suddenly he laughed.

"I only wanted to stretch my legs for half an hour, this being Sunday and our first day ashore. But these martinet Mackintoshes——"

"You'll stretch your legs all right," Ronald said, smiling. "And every Sunday in future you can do exactly as you like. But today we have got to make a home."

He got up and stood beside the pile of stores.

"That's the way we go." He pointed. "Steep at first but better later. If we traversed that basalt over on the left we would reach the other half of the island. . . ."

Ronald talked on to allow Harry time to calm down. He did not mean to give the sharp, unexplained orders which are necessary on a ship. At sea he had obeyed his brother and Bruce like the rest of the crew. But now he

86

had got to assert himself in his own way. Things should go pleasantly, jokingly, without artificial forms of discipline —but exactly as he wanted them to go. "How will you spend your days off, Red? Have you a hobby?"

"I've a hobby all right. But it takes something there ain't 'ere," Red answered with clown-like melancholy.

They laughed and began dividing up the loads.

They carried half loads up to the rim and full loads down to the lagoon. That was the idea. But most of the sacks and boxes, which it was not practicable to divide, weighed at least fifty pounds. And the dinghy and the dredge had to be transported by all four men together. It was killing work in the tropical heat, and it went on all day except for an hour's siesta and the short rests they took after dumping each burden at the camp site. The lagoon with its green margins and dominating mountain was a picture of colourful beauty. But they only thought of it as the place where each carry ended. Stretching their limbs for a few blissful moments, all they appreciated was relief from strain, and a drink of cold water from a spring.

During their many journeys they got to know every detail of the way—the place on the ascent where Geoffrey had slipped flat on his face and marked the rock with the blood of his nose—the place where thorn bushes caught at them—where it was necessary to crawl, the tortoise track being a tunnel through undergrowth—the spot where they could hear the gurgle of a spring—and many more. Monkeys chattered at them from the trees and sometimes threw down sticks. Bright-plumaged birds flashed across their path. On several occasions they met giant tortoises. These last they noticed—they could not avoid doing so because they got in the way. But they noticed little else.

They had been made almost as blind and passive as snails by the sweat on their faces and the loads which weighed them down.

There was one flash of spirit—again from Harry. Late in the afternoon but while the heat was still heavy to bear, he and Ronald were momentarily together in the cove beside what remained of the pile of stores. Ronald picked up one of the three flour sacks which had been submerged in the cutter's boat.

"What's the good of taking these? They are spoiled," Harry said. He kicked a sack, making no more impression than on a rock.

"The flour will be all right inside," Ronald said, and started up the slope.

Half-way he paused to rest, body hooped, hands on the ground, sweat falling from his forehead like water from a dripping tap.

Harry overtook him with both the remaining sacks across his shoulders.

Ronald smiled contentedly.

When at last the final load had been carried to the side of the lagoon all four men, without any of them making the suggestion, slipped off their clothes and went into the water. They swam lazily at first. It was sunset. The surface of the lake was still and as full of colours as an oil-film. The green slopes were becoming black and depth-less. The summit of the mountain on which a purple ray still glowed shimmered with the short flights of birds finding their roosting places.

The men turned upon their backs and watched the stars jump out. The water, which as night comes on develops a special magic, caressed their naked limbs, smoothing away the stiffness and the strain, making them feel light and wonderfully clean. And young. One of them began to kick, sending up a fountain of phosphorescence. The others copied him. Suddenly they began to play like children, splashing, ducking each other, laughing, gasping, shouting.

At last they swam ashore. Groping about in the dark, they gathered armfuls of leaves. They put on a few clothes, ate some biscuits, had a last drink of spring water, and lay down side by side. A few small birds were still twittering in the branches. A monkey scolded. Gradually the sounds died to silence. They slept.

3

The first morning—every morning for that matter— started with sunrise on the mountain-top. That gave the fishers just enough time for getting up and washing, for swallowing a light breakfast and being ready for work before it was sunrise at camp level. Then the dinghy was put into the water and the dredge loaded. Three men rowed out on to the lagoon.

One stayed ashore. He was housekeeper for the day. He had risen at least half an hour earlier than the others to light a cooking fire. His first duty after breakfast was to tidy up the camp site. Then, every morning after the first, he had to deal with the shells which had been opened the evening before. With mother-of-pearl shell selling at up to two hundred pounds a ton it would clearly be worth while to substitute the *Loch Corron*'s ballast for shell if the weather were calm enough when the cutter returned. The housekeeper's duty was to separate the two halves of the shell—this could only be done safely after the hinge had dried—then to clean the shells of growths and barnacles and carry them over to the cove where they were stacked ready for loading on to the ship. A pair of shells weighed five or six pounds, so after a good day's haul the housekeeper had a large number of portage journeys to make.

He never had time to transport all the shell in the morning, for he was expected to put in some work on the shelter which was to house their stores and themselves in rainy weather. And he had to prepare lunch. This involved catching it first, for the stores which they had brought with them were principally intended for emergencies. They had fish lines and a gill net. Having little time to discover where the fish lay they caught little, but they got a few fish which were at least remarkably beautiful before they were cooked. No shooting was done. The only gun— a single-barrelled twelve bore—belonged to Geoffrey, and all but fifty cartridges were found to have been spoiled by dampness during the first part of the voyage. The other weapons were rifles which had been brought as defence against pirates on the voyage or any possible hostile raiders on the island. They were not to be used for ordinary purposes.

Doves could easily have been killed with a stick when they came to the water-holes. This Ronald would not allow, for the doves had been his particular friends during his former visit to the island. But perhaps partly because he had been bred among farmers he was less sentimental about pigeons. There were large numbers of these birds, living wild and apart among the cliffs and caves which bordered the ocean. They were greedy for grain, and it being early summer there was none on the island. Maize brought on the ship was soaked in rum and set out in bowls. The pigeons gorged themselves upon it and thereafter behaved in a most unseemly manner. They died happy, and in consequence were all the better to eat.

There were still eggs in the nests. Some which looked and tasted remarkably like those sold in London as plovers' eggs could be taken from the rock shelves of the mountain. It was never necessary to climb any height, but the collection took time. It also took time to gather fruit in sufficient quantities, for not many sorts were mature at that season.

The housekeeper fed the pearl-fishers at midday. Then he carried the remaining loads of shell to the cove. As soon as that was finished it was time to start thinking of the evening meal. The pearl-fishers were exacting. They expected their meals to be ready and adequate.

For their work was exhausting. The dredges proved efficient, the largest and heaviest being the best because these oysters were so much bigger than the European type. To tow this dredge—as heavy as a harrow—along the bottom of the lagoon meant very hard rowing. To pull it up was a tug-of-war. Besides, since the little boat could not hold any quantity of shells, constant visits to the shore to unload were necessary—all this under a roasting sun with never a chance of shade.

There were plenty of oysters. They could be seen with a water telescope or often with the naked eye since the water was so clear. Even when they happened to be partly buried in the sand they gave themselves away by suddenly closing—presumably alarmed by vibrations caused by the boat—and emitting a little column of bubbles.

But in fact it was not necessary to prospect for the shell. Even when fishing blind the trawl rarely came up empty. So the fishers trawled all day—to and fro, to and fro—marking out with buoys the area they had covered.

An hour before sunset they returned to a place on the shore at some distance from the camp site. Here the housekeeper joined them and together they opened the shells taken during the day. This was an unalterable ceremony, something of a rite. The four men sat round the pile of oysters, opening one after another with large broad-bladed knives. They felt through the contents carefully. Pearls—when there were any—might be in the flesh, or between the flesh and the shell, or attached to the mother-of-pearl. Often they were in the hinge of the shell. Sometimes they were more or less buried by a nacreous covering and had to be cut out. Sometimes—generally in the case of the finest specimens—they were hidden in a caul inside the oyster.

Although there was no individual advantage, there naturally developed a sense of rivalry as to which of them should find the best lot of pearls each evening. So the greasy fingers worked carefully, the heads were bowed, the faces intent as they peered into the plates of mother-of-pearl. Meanwhile the sunset looked at its fading image in the mirror of the lagoon, and ten thousand birds came streaming from the mountain to hover and dive and swerve and race away with a supper of oyster meat.

The work was always followed by a swim. Supper was eaten by lamplight. Ronald's single extravagance had been to bring plenty of lamp-oil so that they could sit up as long as they liked to read or otherwise employ themselves. He had experienced the slavery of depending entirely upon sunlight and the penury of being without books. They had all brought books, except Red. These they would exchange and discuss. Harry was the principal discusser. He would make the most outrageous statements —as often as not personal and rude—merely for the sake of provoking an argument. He thrived on argument. He exercised his brain and the brains of all of them as a gymnastic instructor exercises a class.

He was just as energetic physically. After supper he frequently borrowed the dinghy and went out alone. He had a passion for caves, of which there were many round the lake. He examined them, by diving when he could not row into them. However late he returned he expected the others to be awake and prepared to listen to the account of his adventures.

He was trying to find the connection of the lagoon with the open ocean. That ambition satisfied, he was going ot climb the mountain. He was sure that he could get up and down it within an hour.

Once, soon after Harry had returned to camp, they heard a strange noise in the woods near-by—something like cackling laughter. They peered in its direction, but the lamplight made them blind to everything beyond its circle.

"A bird suddenly waking," Ronald said.

"That weren't no bird, it was a creature," Red corrected.

"A creature unknown to science," Geoffrey murmured. He was half asleep.

"That is not such an absurd statement as you evidently meant it to be," Harry said. "In a sheltered, utterly lonely place like this it is conceivable that one might find an animal which is elsewhere extinct."

"Sorry to disappoint you," Ronald said, "but I explored this island very thoroughly when I was here before, and I found nothing stranger than the giant tortoises."

"I can't believe that you had time to explore thoroughly," Harry said. "One man alone must spend most of his time preparing food. I'm certain you never explored the caves. The island is honeycombed with them. This is a lost world."

"It's lost all right," said Red.

Red had no particular pastime outside working hours. Although a poor swimmer, he enjoyed his bathe as much as anyone. That and supper finished, he would lie on his back and smoke and doze and occasionally burst into song. But if Ronald asked him to help with some repair work he would grumblingly do more than he was asked.

Geoffrey could not splice and mend—or only in a land-lubbery way. And he was always much too tired in the evenings to think of going off exploring as Harry did. Besides reading and telling anecdotes his only recreation was to treacle some trees and catch moths.

"Are you fond of those creatures?" Harry asked him.

"Yes indeed," he said.

"Then why do you kill them?"

"Well . . . From their point of view they die so soon that it makes little difference. From the higher, the artistic point of view practically nobody would get a chance to appreciate their beauty unless I set them with open wings, poised them against a suitable background, and painted their portraits. Do you think I am wantonly destructive?"

"I am not interested in moral questions," Harry said.

94

"But just now you used the word artistic. Do you consider that what you paint is art?"

"What do you consider it?"

"Very neat. Very competent. But no more than scientific illustration. I would like to see a picture which conveys our existence on this island as Frith's 'Derby Day' conveys contemporary English life. But I suppose I ask too much."

Geoffrey did not answer. He felt challenged. But he had at the moment practical worries. It was then Friday night and he would be housekeeper next day. To make certain of having the kettle boiling in time for breakfast—for he was bad at getting up—he collected a good quantity of dry sticks. Thorough and painstaking, he graded these according to size and arranged them in three neat piles beside the cooking fire. The 'kitchen' was near the spring, where there were rocks, thirty or forty yards from the soft and level place where they slept.

When he went to light his fire next morning he found that the sticks had been scattered far and wide. It took a long time to recover enough of them in the grey light.

"Bad fairies," Harry said when Geoffrey made his excuse for breakfast being late.

"Monkeys," said Ronald. "Or a tortoise. They never look where they are going. Or most likely a bird. They are still nesting. I heard some bien-te-veo chattering before you woke. Yes, it was a bird."

"An early bird," said Red.

Geoffrey was not quite satisfied. But he was not going to accuse one of his companions of playing a bad practical joke on him. They laughed at his precise and tidy ways, but he would not go as far as that. The bird which

95

Ronald called a bien-te-veo had many of the mischievous characteristics of a magpie. It might have scattered the sticks.

He worked particularly hard for the rest of the day. He tried not only to produce good food but to serve it attractively, a refinement which nobody had yet attempted. He added some artistic touches to the shelter which was nearing completion. Also he improved the bedding place, making a rest of plaited branches against which they could lean their backs when sitting up.

Ronald praised the result.

"I don't do much," Geoffrey said.

The two men were alone in camp, the others swimming.

Ronald said, "When Mr. Pinkerton told me that I must take a man of his I very nearly revolted—until I discovered whom he was referring to. When I did—and ever since—I have felt that Pinkerton was my guardian angel, rather well disguised."

Geoffrey glowed and protested.

"I am not as strong as the others."

"You spent too much time being sea-sick on the voyage. You will soon pick up. But—what is more important to me—if there ever was any trouble you are the one whose advice I would naturally depend on."

Ronald watched the swimmers for a moment. Then he added, "I look on you as my second-in-command."

Geoffrey was exhilarated. Later—preparing supper which refused to cook as he meant it to—it occurred to him that the compliment might have been more friendly than sincere. Ronald's keen eyes had seen that he was down and needed encouragement. But he found that he could not believe that explanation. Ronald had too strict a regard for truth. He did not hand out compliments like tots of rum.

Later in the evening, when they were all together after supper, Ronald remarked that if he himself should ever suffer an accident, Geoffrey would take over.

No one spoke. Red, lying on his back, blew a smoke ring. Harry with a boxer's blow knocked it into spinning shreds.

Ronald took from his pocket the pickle bottle which contained the pearls. He poured them out on to a blanket. There was a good number of them, for besides those collected during the last six days there were those which Ronald had left behind in a cache on his first visit to the island. They made a glowing constellation on the blanket.

The men began to count them, and to wonder how many more they would collect in three months.

4

They had previously agreed that there would be no house-keeping on Sunday. It would be every man for himself as far as meals were concerned. But while too many cooks were spoiling breakfast Ronald said that he would be responsible for supper.

"No, I'll do it," Geoffrey said. "I have no particular plans—only to paint a picture."

"If it is as good as the canvas I will humbly retract my disparagement of your artistic gifts," Harry said.

The canvas had been a joke the night before. Geoffrey had found a suitable piece of cloth among the stores. But it had proved very difficult to stretch it taut. To make a sufficiently rigid frame—he was no carpenter—he had to employ four two-foot sticks as thick as his arm. Over this he stretched the canvas, lacing it behind with string and tacking it to the rim. But even then it was not tight enough, and he had to use more wood as wedges. This had employed him until midnight. The result was a rustic-looking creation weighing some twenty pounds.

Ronald said he intended to spend the day above the cove, improving the path in the steepest places.

Harry asked leave to borrow the dinghy. He believed that the likeliest places for the water connection to come out into the lagoon were close to the mountain—either on the shore where they were encamped or on the opposite side. He wanted to make a reconnaissance by day-light.

Red had no plans.

They pocketed something to eat at midday, and parted.

About three hundred yards from camp Geoffrey found a perfect natural studio. On the lakeside near the mountain the trees grew thickly, giving shade to the artist and at the same time permitting him sufficient view. He was too close to the mountain to include it in his picture. But it was too tall for that in any case. He intended to suggest its height by its reflection in the water. That he could not see the camp did not disturb him. He knew what it looked like and would put it in somewhere else. It was a general impression he was after, not accurate detail.

He spent half an hour rigging up an easel in proportion to his canvas. Then he started work. From the first moment he was happy. He let himself go in splashing enough colour on to the canvas to match the scene in front

98

of him. It was a wonderful relaxation from the photographic precision necessary in painting insects.

When he grew hungry he retired a few paces and sat with his back against the nearest tree, munching and admiring. It was all there—the boat with the fishers bending over the dredge, Harry swimming, the lonely camp, the monkeys, the tortoises. The whole story of island life was written there, although so far only in a sort of shorthand form. He went back to finish it off.

So absorbed was he that it came as a shock to realise from the changing colours that it was already evening. He had not quite finished yet, but he must not rush the end. He left the picture propped against a tree and climbed a little way up the mountain to collect a dozen sea birds' eggs. Then he hurried back to camp to prepare supper.

Only Red was there. He looked thoroughly miserable. He had the "'ell of an 'eadache".

"You shouldn't sleep in the sun," Geoffrey said cheerfully.

"I didn't. I chose a bit of shade particular. But the sun moved."

Geoffrey laughed.

"It's all right for you," Red said crossly. "But what is there for a normal fellow to do in this benighted 'ole?"

For once he really was in a bad temper and resented having his leg pulled.

Geoffrey left him to himself and lit the fire.

The next arrival was Ronald. He looked like a man who had worked hard in the sun all day. He had drunk no more than the bottle of water he had taken with him. He was desperately thirsty and evidently tired.

"How did you two enjoy yourselves?" he asked when he had recovered a little.

99

Red only grunted.

Geoffrey said that he had started his picture. "But it will be a day or two before I can submit it to the hanging committee."

In fact the picture only needed another hour's work and he intended to finish it at lunch-time next day. But he would keep it hidden where it was until then.

He beat up the eggs. They were a beautiful orange colour. His twelve-egg omelette would be another work of art. But he could not make it until they were all assembled.

At last Harry came into view rowing along the edge of the lake from the direction of the mountain. He strode into camp. They asked if he had found the connection.

"No. I wasted the whole day. I can't think where the damned thing is." He laughed his quick bark of a laugh.

"But I came on something else," he said. "Geoffrey's picture."

Geoffrey flushed and waited for the verdict.

"Is supper ready yet?" Harry asked.

"In one minute," Geoffrey moved to the fire.

He heard Ronald ask, "What's it like?"

The answer was whispered. He heard no more of the conversation except, "You'll see for yourself tomorrow." After that they were all silent.

Directly he had served out the omelette, which was burnt, Geoffrey strolled away, saying he was not hungry. When he was out of sight he began to run.

The picture was smudged and blurred, the colours rubbed into each other.

He flung the thing into the lake and walked away. It was already getting dark among the trees. He stumbled over obstacles. Creepers scratched his face. He strode on blindly.

What a beastly thing to do! If Harry was as spiteful as that it was a bad look-out for the future.

Geoffrey wandered for an hour before he felt calm enough to go back to camp and maintain his reputation for even temper.

5

Monday started the week's work busily and well. Immediately everyone was in a good temper again. Handling the dredge, Red was absorbed as an artist. He excelled them all in this skill, and knew it. They could pull his leg as much as they liked. He answered with dry humour, generally getting the better of the exchange. In any case he was never offended.

"This is not such a bad hole after all," Geoffrey said.

"It's all right for *work*."

Red stood with his carrot hair on end, his red face clashing with it, his chest puffed out, his arms held slightly away from his body as a fighting-cock holds its wings.

"There are other things besides work," he said, very solemnly.

Harry argued with Geoffrey on all sorts of subjects, as friendly as a boxer with his sparring partner. Geoffrey was still deeply hurt about the picture, but this he managed to conceal. If you have got to live at close quarters with someone for a long time you might as well live amicably.

And he could not avoid admiring Harry. He was widely read in a variety of subjects. He appeared to know quite a lot about geology. He could quote poetry by the hour. He appreciated music. But chiefly Geoffrey envied his energy. When fishing there were periods of comparative repose. Harry used these to dive on his own account.

Ronald asked why he did it.

"I get up a few more shells. You should not complain," Harry answered.

"I'm not complaining. I just wonder why you do it. You have never shown any great interest in pearls."

Harry laughed.

"Swimming under water is entirely a matter of practice. I want to be able to go deep."

Ronald pointed out that except in a few places they knew the lake to be shallow. What was the point of going deep?

"If you hammer a big blunt nail into a piece of wood it cracks it wide and deep," Harry said. "When that basalt plug was pushed up it may have caused cracks all around it. You see what I am getting at. We know that the ocean outside is very deep. This island is the top of a mountain, perhaps twenty or thirty thousand feet high, rising steeply from the ocean depths. That's my theory anyway. There may be deep cracks in the limestone, one or more of which goes right through to the ocean."

"What about searching on land, charting the position of the blow-holes. If you could find two in line——"

"I've thought of that. The blow-holes can have nothing to do with it. They have been blown out of limited caves when the air was compressed by waves. The cave which goes right through would have no need to blow out a safety-valve. I can't search for it on the ocean side. This lagoon is the place to explore foot by foot."

"Don't go swimming into caves. You might not be able to get out. No risks. That's an order," Ronald said, with the mixture of lightness and authority which Geoffrey admired. He himself would have obeyed any suggestion of his leader, let alone an order.

Harry did not appear to be impressed. He continued to practise diving by day and to go off by himself at night. But during the first half of the week he returned early and there were no incidents. Geoffrey wondered if he had become discouraged and only continued his explorations to show his independence outside working hours. After all, if the connection were with the deep ocean levels he had no hope of finding it. Harry must have realised that.

"Why don't you climb the mountain?" Geoffrey asked him.

"All in good time," said Harry.

On Thursday Geoffrey was again housekeeper. Red, who had preceded him, had left over a number of pigeons. For supper Geoffrey decided to make a pigeon pie. It was an ambitious but not impossible plan. Ronald had made an oven. It was a question of whether he himself could make pastry. As a boy he had often watched the family cook making it.

He rolled out the paste with a length of smooth stick, covered the filled dish and put it in the oven. Then he tried to resist the constant temptation to peep in and see if the pastry was rising.

When the fishers returned he helped with the oyster opening. But instead of bathing with the others he returned to the cooking fire.

Twenty minutes later the pie was baked. Although not perfect it was recognisable for what it was meant to be. He allowed himself a little recreation.

He stood on the slope above the shore, watching the bathers. Two of them had come out of the water and were walking about on the shore while they dried. Although most of the area of their bodies had become sun-tanned on the voyage, the parts which they kept clothed had not. They bathed naked, but almost invariably when the sun had set or lost its burning power. It was the hour when white looks whitest and the piebald bodies offended his artistic eye. They were like plants grown in a cellar exposed among garden flowers. He looked away.

From where he stood the mountain was on the left, making a fairly straight side to the lake. Elsewhere the low shore curved round in a three-quarter circle. The vegetation which grew on it was darkening with the ebb of light. Geoffrey's eyes swept round this curve. He started violently, and stared.

Near the distant shore, close to the place where the furthest buttress of the mountain cut into the low-lying limestone, he had seen a flash. Phosphorescence. But that meant that something was breaking the surface.

It was more than one glow of light. There were many. They seemed to form a pattern, spreading to a sinuous line, then closing up.

"Ronald. Red, Harry. Come here! Come quick!"

They obeyed the excitement in his voice. He pointed. They stood naked beside him. He pointed.

"Cor! A sea serpent," Red exclaimed in awe.

"I can't make out if it is one creature or more," Ronald said. "I wish it did not get dark so quickly."

"I'm going to have a look," Harry said, and started for the shore.

"Harry!" Ronald called sharply.

Harry stopped, but only turned his head.

'Oh Lord,' thought Geoffrey, 'I have caused a crisis. He will never obey.'

"We will all go and look," Ronald said. "Get the boat into the water while I fetch a rifle."

Ronald steered. The rowers watched his face in the starlight. "Still there?" they kept asking.

"Yes."

The panting of the rowers became louder, but the creak and splash of oars kept an even rhythm.

Ronald stood up.

"Still there?"

"No. It's vanished."

"Where?"

"It's impossible to judge in this light. Somewhere near the shore."

"Not on to the shore—or into a cave?"

"The phosphorescence vanished. That's all I'm certain of."

"Let's keep going. It may have dived. It might come up again."

They reached the further shore without seeing any trace of whatever it had been. They waited and watched until their necks were stiff with turning. After half an hour they rowed back, close under the mountain where they knew the water was deep. Ronald had transferred to the bow. He crouched there, rifle in hand.

They went slowly, talking now and then.

"Do you think it was a single large creature or a number

of smaller ones keeping together?" Harry asked.

They answered that they thought a single creature.

"I don't agree. I believe that if Red had not said 'serpent' you would never have thought of it. When he did, your imagination made everything serpentine."

"I know a sea serpent when I see one," Red grumbled.

"I believe it was a school of porpoises. They often keep formation," Harry said.

"Call them mermaids," said Red.

"Whatever it was must have come in from the ocean by the connecting cave."

They continued the argument, desultorily, as anyone thought of a new idea. They were impatient with each other's theories. They were tired, hungry and disappointed.

"Quiet! Stop rowing!" Ronald whispered.

The boat drifted silently forward. The rowers looked over their shoulders. There was a white patch on the dark water in front. It was quite different from whatever they had seen on the other side of the lagoon, but they could not make out what this thing was either.

"Two strokes. Quietly."

They obeyed, then waited, not even daring to turn. They heard the click as Ronald cocked his rifle.

"Well I'm—— What is it?"

They looked round. The white thing was rectangular. They paddled up to it.

"Leave it where it is," Geoffrey said. "It's my picture."

"What the devil is it doing there?"

"I threw it into the lagoon. It's no good."

There was a silence. They had their own thoughts about Geoffrey's picture.

"It's at least two hundred yards from where you painted it," Harry broke out excitedly. No one responded, and he went on. "Don't you understand? It has drifted— against any wind there was. The tide is ebbing. It's held here, under our end of the mountain. Look, it's gyrating. The inner end of the connection must be down there."

"It can stay there," said Red. "I want my supper."

Next day Harry was housekeeper. When they returned in the evening they found him still busy in the kitchen. A cooking rivalry had developed between them. He put an excellent meal before them. He said, "*Bon appétit*, I've had something already. I'm going off in the boat."

"No risks!" Ronald said. "You can't get down to that connection."

Harry laughed. "I promise you that I have as much respect for my lungs and my skin as you have. But I've taken no exercise all day. I'll burst if I don't do something."

They had all composed themselves to sleep when he returned, and no one greeted him. This from past experience was not enough to stop him launching into lively talk. But he went to bed very quietly indeed.

Next morning they saw that he had hurt his face. Three deep lines furrowed the length of his left cheek.

"How did you do that?" Ronald asked.

"Scratched it on a bit of rock."

"Rock? Was it coral?"

"Might have been."

"Don't you know that coral is poisonous? Why didn't you wake me last night? Stay where you are."

Harry stayed where he was, sitting up on his bed of leaves, looking as pathetic as a hurt dog. He did not say anything to either Red or Geoffrey.

Ronald returned with the small medicine chest. He damped a swab and began scraping away the scar. Harry bore it quietly. But when disinfectant was applied he cried out in pain.

"Keep still," Ronald said.

"Damn it, what are you trying to do?"

"I have got to get this clean. I tell you coral is poisonous."

Red began to laugh.

Harry shouted, "That's acid you're using. It burns like hell."

"Keep still," Ronald said again, and while he picked and rubbed, he gave Harry a lecture about taking risks. He had no right to hurt himself like that, still less to neglect cleaning a probably poisoned wound.

"You said yourself—only the other day—that you might have an accident," Harry said, catching his breath between each phrase.

"Keep still. I've nearly finished. I would not blame anyone who hurt himself while working."

"Working! I do my share of oyster-mongering."

"There. You'll do now," Ronald said. He shook Harry by the shoulders, and smiled. "You've made me late with breakfast. But it won't be a minute." He went back to the fire.

"Well of all the——" Harry said. He turned to Geoffrey. "Did he really think my face was poisoned, or did he—— What the devil are you laughing at now? Oh, all right, as it so happens I think it's funny myself."

He was unusually silent all day. He seemed to be brooding. Geoffrey, never very sure of his authority, wished that it did not happen to be Ronald's day in camp. But Harry behaved perfectly well and Red was at his best. The fishing was a success.

Ronald met them as they landed and congratulated them on their haul. Then drawing Harry aside, "I will take it as a compliment if you will have supper with us instead of going adventuring tonight."

"Is that an order?" Harry asked.

"Yes."

"But of course I will. What have we got to eat?"

Geoffrey was interested by this overheard conversation, and he could see that Red was too.

During the meal Ronald talked plans for the next day, Sunday. He suggested that Harry would be better equipped if he had a chart of the lake. He offered to help him to make soundings. He had already looked out a hundred fathoms of cord.

"Very well. Thanks," Harry said.

"What about you, Geoffrey?"

"I'm hunting butterflies. I thought of trying the Toe of the island."

"You'll find plenty there."

"Which is the best way to go? Above the cove is steep for me."

"The south side of the lagoon is easier. There's a tortoise track. Behind where we saw the sea serpent. Harry, did you get another glimpse of it last night?"

"It wasn't a sea serpent and I did not see anything," Harry said.

"You were in that corner?"

"Yes. There are a number of little caves; it's fascinating to explore."

"No sort of connection with the sea?"

"No, no. But they go in and down and up again. Under water and out of it. That's where I got held."

"Held? What do you mean?"

"Stuck. It was dark. I could not see or breathe. I thought I was done for. That's where I scratched my face."

Harry shivered. There was fear in his eyes.

6

Geoffrey set off gaily with his green butterfly net and the satchel which contained his lunch and killing-bottle. He was pleased at the prospect of a day by himself. It was absurd, but in this lonely life he never seemed to be alone —except when burdened by the cares of housekeeping. Fishing, they were crowded in the dinghy. Sleeping as they did was equivalent to sharing a room with three people. Harry came in late. Red snored. Ronald sometimes murmured in his sleep. One could not hear what he said, but one could not help trying to. There was no privacy.

But now he was alone, engaged upon the sort of expedition that he most enjoyed. Painting, he was generally too conscious of his limitations—or if he was temporarily unconscious of them he was disappointed afterwards by the result. But butterfly hunting combined sport, science and art in manageable proportions. He was always happy butterflying.

He climbed obliquely up the slope until he reached the rim. He stood there, holding on to his hat with both hands. Down by the lagoon it was nearly always perfectly calm. But here the wind blew hard. Three hundred feet below him the great waves swept in, rank upon rank, and hurled themselves against the cliffs. He remembered Harry saying that the island was a mountain-top. He pictured himself standing on a lofty summit with a sea of clouds hiding the earth below—a cloud of sea hiding the ocean floor.

He turned back towards the lake, following a different track. On the way he caught up with a tortoise going for a drink. He decided to get a lift. It was not a comfortable ride—too wide a saddle—and the big reptile kept stretching its head round and snapping at his legs. He slipped off, raised his hat, and walked on.

He came out on the lagoon shore exactly opposite the mountain. Half left, he could see the position of the camp site. But at the distance of about a mile he could make out no actual detail, not even Red's colourful body. Evidently he had got himself properly into the shade this time.

Geoffrey sat down for a rest. The surveyors were working methodically up and down the lagoon in parallel lines, about a hundred yards apart, sounding as they went. He waved to them. It was pleasant to see them busily engaged while he was idle. But he decided to go on.

He followed the shore round in an anti-clockwise direction. Opposite the camp the bank was between ten and twenty feet high. Underneath him were some caves which Harry had explored. Somewhere off this shore they had seen the strange creature, or creatures.

He was now close to the mountain, and bore away to the right to cross its skirts as low down as possible. The vegetation became thick. He forced his way through it with some difficulty until he came to a tortoise track. This as Ronald had said led between the mountain and the sea-cliff to the other part of the island.

It was the strangest pass he had ever crossed—a tunnel through sparse scrub which gave glimpses of the surging sea below upon the right, and on the left the mountain soaring up, seeming to waver in the cloud of birds. But it had the quality of all passes of opening up a new landscape. This so much interested him that he scrambled some distance up the mountain to get a better view.

The Toe was nearly twice the area of the Heel. And it was much less regular in every way. Instead of being a rim of land framing a central lake, the land predominated. It undulated, had little valleys and gorges and outcroppings of rock. There was a patch of forest over towards the other side. There was a lake—Geoffrey could see the gleam of water through the trees. There was a great deal of varied vegetation—different shades of green. He climbed down to explore.

It was his idea of a perfect garden—large, colourful and full of variety. In one place palm trees held their parasols high overhead. In another was a banana grove. The broad leaves rustled with a noise like that of ice gyrated in a glass. The plants canalised the air. A whispering breeze swung the fruit bunches invitingly in the green shade. There were cliffs down which a tapestry of creepers hung, grottoes and caves where ferns and mosses grew and water dripped, thickets of sugar cane, open swards, a diversity of flowers and fruit. It was rarely possible to see

112

more than fifty yards ahead, and every glimpse from crest or leafy opening was a surprise.

For the best part of an hour Geoffrey wandered in a dream.

Then he saw an *ornithoptera priamus*.

So far that day he had not used his net. He had seen a few butterflies—more or less common species of which he had obtained specimens during his oriental business trip. In any case with noon approaching it had been too hot to run.

But a bird-wing butterfly was a collector's piece. This was a male, so much more beautiful than the female. Its fore-wings were black with a green streak at the edges. Its hind-wings were green with black markings. Its body was brilliant yellow. It had a span, he judged, of six or seven inches—as big as a swallow's. Geoffrey had never seen one of this species before. But of course he had read about them and seen pictures. He knew it as he would have known some world-famous personality. And it was only a few yards away, sunning itself on a leaf.

With every muscle and nerve and drop of blood he became a hunter. Nothing in the world mattered except the capture of that particular insect. He was blind to everything else. He crept forward, intently watching the luxurious yawnings of those lovely wings.

He made his spring. The big butterfly was not in his net. It was lazily and rather clumsily flying away.

He raced after it, dodging round rocks, jumping fallen trees, barging through drooping branches. It paused on a flower. At the last moment it fluttered away. He lost it for an agonising minute, then found it again, once more settled. Again it evaded him. What was particularly maddening was that it appeared unconscious of his existence. It just happened to fly away at the moment when he was about to bring his net down on top of it.

For ten minutes or more this mockery continued. The butterfly fluttered from flower to flower. Geoffrey sprinted or crept. But his net was always a fraction of a second late.

Then the *ornithoptera priamus* flew off on a more constant course, slowly, down a glade. It happened to fly at a height of twelve feet. Geoffrey ran below it. He ran into a bush.

He lost sight of the butterfly—found it again . . . So it went on. The vegetation changed. But he did not notice this—or only in so far as it helped or hindered his chase. He was panting, dripping with sweat, and the bush he had run into had left some thorns in him. But he thought only of the butterfly.

It flew over a thicket of sugar cane. He dived headlong into it, and for agonising seconds struggled with the canes. Something else was in the thicket too, making as much commotion as he was. He emerged suddenly into open ground and his eyes searched for the butterfly. He saw a girl running away from him, a copper-coloured girl with black hair flying and green canes falling from the bundle on her back. Almost at the same moment he saw the butterfly. For a second he hesitated. Then he ran after the girl.

He called out to her. She looked back at him, and ran on. That glance drew him after her as hard as he could go. The ground sloped gently downwards. There were trees among which he was afraid that he might lose her. He ran, still grasping the net in his right hand, his left steadying the bag which contained the killing-bottle. He kept her in sight but was too tired to overtake. He called again, trying to reassure her, to persuade her to stop.

She stopped, her arms about the trunk of an orange tree, her body bent, her head turned to watch him coming on. Then off she went again in a slightly different direction. To the left he saw a low line of cliffs. In front and to the right was the gleam of water. He felt that the race would end at the water's edge unless she had time to double back. He put on a sprint.

Suddenly the ground fell steeply to a green bowl between the cliff and a lake. A number of people were sitting about in groups. They rose and converged. They were women. The running girl raced to them and they closed about her.

Chapter Five

Geoffrey's legs carried him on. He could not stop before he was at the bottom of the bowl, among the women. He stood gasping.

From somewhere in the background a voice spoke, sharply, giving an order. A man's voice. The women began to move away, some fast, some slowly, looking over their shoulders. They were young and their skins were of different shades. Only one stood her ground beside the man who was now apparent as a man although he wore a strange loose garment. He gave another order and the flock of girls disappeared one by one into the cliff.

The man advanced on Geoffrey. When he was about five yards away he suddenly stopped. He stared.

"It's you, Mr. Partridge," he said.

Geoffrey, out of breath and completely bewildered, continued to gasp.

"You do not recognise me?"

The man had come slowly forward again until he was close to Geoffrey. He was regarding him attentively but with just a hint of quizzical humour. The expression was familiar. And the pose—leaning slightly forward, the eyes raised as if looking over spectacles.

"Skinner," said Geoffrey, although without conviction.

"That's right! How are you, Mr. Partridge?"

Geoffrey took the extended hand and said nothing.

"You did not recognise me," Skinner said. "But it is just as much of a surprise for me, sir. It never entered my head that you might be one of the pearl-fishers by the lagoon."

'So Skinner knew about the party and what they were doing,' Geoffrey thought. 'Of course he would. Skinner invariably knew everything.'

"You and I must have a good talk, Mr. Partridge. We have always understood each other very well, if I may say so."

They were walking slowly side by side towards the woman who had stood her ground. She wore a sarong. As he came closer Geoffrey saw that she had something of the Malayan cast of countenance, but that her skin was strikingly pale. It was stretched tightly over the bony structure of her face. A mane of black hair swept back from her low, broad forehead. Her dark eyes were fixed intently upon him, but without expression.

"This is Mr. Partridge, a good friend from my own country," Skinner said to her. He turned to Geoffrey. "My partner, Silver."

Geoffrey wondered if he ought to shake hands. But the woman was now looking at Skinner.

"Mr. Partridge will have luncheon with me out here," Skinner said. "You can stay, Mr. Partridge? Please do. But before that I believe he would like a long drink."

The woman turned and walked away.

"If you are not still too overheated perhaps you would care to take a dip," Skinner said.

The polite formality of the remark made Geoffrey suddenly conscious of the mess that he was in—shirt out of his shorts and sticking to his skin, sweat making channels down his dusty legs.

"Oh yes, thanks very much," he said.

"Will you come this way, sir? Our lake is rather shallow for swimming. But the water is fresh and clean."

At a short distance along the shore was a grove of bamboos. Parting the stems with his hands Skinner showed that a horse-shoe-shaped space had been cleared, bordering on the water. There was a rough bench, a cupboard and a sort of dressing-table.

"This is the place I use myself," Skinner said. "Towel, mirror, comb, soap—only home-made soap, I am afraid, but you will find it lathers quite well. Is there anything else you require? Then I will leave you."

When Geoffrey left the grove he saw Skinner standing beside a low table under a big, solitary tree which grew near the cliff. There was no one else about. Refreshed and clear-headed after his wash, he found it difficult to believe he had seen a score of exotically dressed young women. He looked at the cliff and saw the mouth of a cave. It was screened by creepers which hung down like a curtain.

"Try some of our home brew," Skinner said.

From a gourd container he filled a cup made from a coconut shell. Geoffrey, who was extremely thirsty, drank it at a draught.

"Delicious!" he exclaimed.

"It is a distillation of the juice of the palm tree. Some of my people are highly skilled at that sort of thing," Skinner said.

118

"Your people——?"

Skinner who had been refilling the cup went on. "Yes, we have made wine too. But I do not think it can yet be matured. So I thought it best to offer you this. You really like it?"

"It is so wonderfully cool. It is a long time since I have had a really cold drink."

"Ah, that is the cave. The inner recesses make a perfect cellar. You shall see it after lunch—which will be ready any minute. Will you sit down?"

Fibre mats had been spread beside the low table. Geoffrey lay on his side, his head propped up by a forearm, and sipped cold coconut punch. It was very pleasant in the shade of the tree, a gentle breeze coming from the lake. The imperturbable Skinner was making small talk. He had explained nothing, but presumably he would in his own time. Geoffrey remembered that it had never been possible to hurry Skinner.

"Are you here for long, Mr. Partridge?"

"For three months—well, it is only about two and a half months longer now—that is if we get enough pearls in the time," Geoffrey said.

"No doubt you will," Skinner said politely. "By the way, what is that dredge you are using?"

Geoffrey told him.

"And it works well? How interesting. I dare say it would on such a smooth bottom. Was it your own idea, Mr. Partridge?"

"No, it was Ronald Mackintosh's. He is the leader and organiser," Geoffrey said, and stopped short.

"Please do not think me inquisitive," Skinner said. "But I am naturally interested in your party as you must be in mine, since fate has brought us both to this lonely island. Needless to say, anything you tell me will go no further. And for my part I will ask you to promise not to repeat anything I shall tell you—not to mention our meeting. That settled, we can talk frankly to our mutual advantage. After all, we know each other well and trust each other. Is that not so?"

Geoffrey agreed. Then, little by little, prompted by Skinner's questions, he told how the expedition had been planned and equipped. He explained his own inclusion in the party.

"I was enormously surprised at Pinkerton putting up fifteen hundred pounds after only one talk with Ronald Mackintosh. The whole thing was most odd. Pinkerton had all the clerks searching for an old report. They never found it, but Pinkerton seemed to know a lot about the island."

"Did he tell you that he had been here?" Skinner asked, a strange light in his eyes.

"No. But he knew about the lack of an anchorage, and that the ocean was deep. He said that we would probably fish out the lagoon fairly quickly. I gathered that was why he was glad to leave the responsibility and organising to Mackintosh instead of trying to take over the island for the firm."

Skinner smiled and nodded. Geoffrey went on talking. At the back of his mind was the thought that the more he told, the more he could hope to be told by Skinner in return. There was a great deal he wanted to know.

Lunch was served to them by Silver. They ate from roughly made wooden dishes, with wooden spoons and forks. But the food was excellent. The first dish consisted of rice and fish, but was full of unexpected flavours. The second was meat and various fruits wrapped up together. Geoffrey remarked how good it was.

"It is a Tahitian dish," Skinner told him. "The food is wrapped in leaves and cooked between hot stones with a covering of earth to prevent the steam escaping—most ingenious."

"You have an international kitchen."

"Not only the kitchen. I always intended that my people should, if I may so put it, constitute the many and various volumes of an encylopædia on the art of living. But you were telling me about your own commissariat. Please go on."

Silver sometimes paused by the table for a minute or two, as if to see that the men had all they needed. She was silent and attentive, but not always expressionless. Once when Geoffrey was talking about their plans he glanced up suddenly and surprised a look of concern, almost of fear, on her face.

"You have done me wonderfully well," he said when a basket of fruit, and pipes and tobacco had been put upon the table and Silver had withdrawn. "Your organising skill is as amazing as ever."

"A Sunday luncheon," said Skinner with his deferential smile.

"But you did not expect me."

"No," Skinner said, all at once serious, "I did not expect anyone. And I do not want visitors—apart from you, Mr. Partridge. I am going to ask you to add something to your promise. Will you do your best to prevent your companions from visiting this part of the island?"

Geoffrey, taken aback by the sudden change of mood, was silent.

"It will be best from every point of view," Skinner went on. "If the two parties should meet, the work of both would be disturbed."

"Yes, I suppose it would," Geoffrey said.

"I never doubted that you would agree. But had I been talking to someone less intelligent than yourself, Mr. Partridge—someone who did not agree—I must tell you that I would stop at nothing to prevent interference with my creation of Heaven upon Earth."

Geoffrey's mouth opened, but he said nothing.

"I have been planning this ideal state for more than a quarter of a century, and for the last two and a half years have been actively putting it into effect. A busy, useful, productive Heaven."

"Please, Skinner! For goodness' sake explain," Geoffrey said. "How did you come here? Who are your people? What is this Heaven on Earth you are creating?"

"It is a perfectly simple idea, Mr. Partridge. Everybody has his private dream, his secret picture of an ideal life. But I do not think that one person in ten million ever imagines that it could come true. I was the exception. I refused to believe it was impossible. I strove continually to make my dream a reality. Would you care to stroll round and see something of the result?" Skinner asked, rising to his feet.

"I would indeed," said Geoffrey.

Along the shore of the lake, beyond Skinner's bathing place, there were a number of tiny buildings, constructed of a variety of materials, all different, strikingly individual.

"My people's castles," Skinner said with his strange, fleeting smile. "You know—an Englishman's home is his castle. Why only an Englishman's? The need is universal. Everybody should have their private place to which they can retire, a place in every sense their own—you look surprised——"

"I was just wondering if liberty—too much liberty—might not be dangerous."

Skinner looked at Geoffrey with the expression which he could not decipher as serious or joking.

"My design, as I have said, is Heaven upon Earth. Do you not feel that liberty is a necessary ingredient?"

"Oh yes, of course. But—well, you have to make them work, I suppose."

"We work very hard. That is another ingredient of happiness."

They walked on in silence. Soon they reached the farm. Only a few acres were fully cultivated—with rice, maize, tobacco, vegetables and other crops. Other areas were more or less cleared.

"I suppose you have turned all the ground by hand," Geoffrey said.

Skinner nodded. "There was an enormous amount of manual labour to be done—felling the trees, drawing the roots, removing stones, turning the earth with home-made spades. It was a slow process, but thorough, a long-term investment." He talked with increasing enthusiasm. The future farm was clear in his mind, neat, efficient, scientifically planned. He described it while Geoffrey looked at the wild profusion of tropical vegetation, at rocks which seemed as if they had been where they were at the beginning of the world and meant to stay there till the end.

Further towards the Toe of the island were enclosures of livestock—pigs, goats, turkeys, chickens, geese.

"Some of these survived the landing," Skinner said. "Others were caught here while they were quite young."

"What do you feed them on?"

"The grain and vegetables we grow. It is a much more precise and complicated problem to run a farm here than in England."

"How is that? I should have thought things grow better here," Geoffrey said. Farming was not one of his interests, but Skinner's radiating enthusiasm had infected him.

"The problem is to grow the right proportions of flora and fauna, if you see what I mean. In England it does not matter what one produces so long as there is enough to sell. There cannot be too much of anything marketable. But here there is no market. We produce only for ourselves. Too much grain, fruit, vegetables waste the ground. Excess animals require food which otherwise need not have been produced."

"Surely there is enough land to allow a margin of extravagance," Geoffrey said.

"At present, yes. But I am working out a formula for the future when all the ground will be needed."

"You do the work yourself?"

"I plan. Silver is my lieutenant, my foreman—in charge of discipline and detail. The rest of my people do the manual labour—on the farm, in the workshops, in the household."

"I don't see any of them about," Geoffrey said.

"Oh no, this is Sunday afternoon."

"What do your people do on Sunday?"

"Anything they like—within limits, of course. They used to enjoy bathing in the lagoon. Most of them were born beside the sea, and the open sea is of course too rough and difficult to reach. Today—I dare say they are in the cave, doing handicrafts and so on. Each individual has a spare-time hobby, and a working responsibility. That is one of the secrets of happiness."

"You seem to have everything very well worked out. How long have you been here?" Geoffrey asked.

"Just over a year."

"How did you manage to get ashore—I mean with women."

Skinner smiled, "I believe, Mr. Partridge, that your ideas of young ladies must be coloured by those whom you have met at home. Most of mine can swim better than any Englishman I have met—some of them are exceptionally good. That was a prime factor in their selection. They thought nothing of plunging through the breakers. In fact it was they who dragged me ashore." He smiled.

"But your stores?"

"We brought very few. We have made what we needed. I have experts in everything."

"You cannot have made everything—the clothing, for instance."

"That did not amount to much bulk. As for the rest, I will show you the workshops in a minute."

The 'workshops' were a couple of roughly constructed sheds. But in them corn was ground and the raw products of the coconut palm were processed to produce oil, fibre, wax and wine.

"Your people can do all this work?" Geoffrey asked.

"Oh, yes."

125

"But aren't they—I mean, they must be highly trained."

"They have been brought up from childhood in their various skills. They are young and intelligent. I give them general instruction and Silver supervises them closely."

"Silver must be a remarkable person," Geoffrey said.

"She is indeed. She is the daughter of a Malayan princess and an English merchant adventurer, a fine old fellow with a white beard that used to stab at your chest while he talked to you. I met him and the princess on my first visit to the East. Silver was a tiny baby then. Her father named her after his ship, the Silver Dream. She was brought up partly at sea, partly with a highly respectable white family who saw to her schooling, and partly on her mother's island in the Sulu Sea. A sufficiently varied upbringing! But the result is a person who has the best qualities of both white and coloured. I really don't know what I should do without her. I would have found it very difficult to put my plans into operation without her aid."

Skinner sat down on the trunk of a small tree which had been uprooted in the process of cultivation. He crossed one leg over the other and rubbed his knee.

"I hurt it the other day," he said. "Nothing at all. But it gets tired. Do you mind if we rest a few minutes?"

"Mind? I would enjoy it. Particularly if you go on telling me how one organises a Heaven on Earth—as you used to instruct me on the workings of Pinkerton and Powell."

"This, if I may say so, is better organised," Skinner said. "Where shall I begin?"

"At the beginning. How does one recruit the staff?"

Skinner chuckled.

"You are a tonic, Mr. Partridge. You are quite right to stress the importance of what you call my staff. That was my first consideration when I had obtained the necessary capital. I had worked out what I wanted to achieve. But I had to find the right assistants. Choosing staff depends partly on your own powers of discernment—of reading character—and partly upon chance. In all I have achieved I must acknowledge chance as my kindest patron. I was able to offer security, interest, freedom. I have learned to judge character. But as I travelled about in the guise of a tourist it was mainly chance which enabled me to pick the right people for my purpose.

"My first voyage after commissioning my brig—my first experiment in navigation, which I had studied more in theory than in practice—was to the island in the Sulu Sea which Silver's mother had ruled twenty-five years before. The Ranee had aged greatly and the old order had changed. The place could not keep up with the times. The bearded buccaneer had died somewhere far away. But the child he had called Silver Dream—I told her about my plans. She was interested. I was interested in her. I could see her qualities——"

"Silver was the first of your people?"

"In more senses than one. But I left her in her strange kingdom for another year. I could not have found the number I required there, let alone the varieties of skills. I had much preparatory work to do. I picked Silver up with the most suitable of her personal women just before starting for the island."

"Were all those girls I saw outside the cave her personal women?"

"Oh dear, no. Only a few of them. The rest came from

all sorts of different countries. That was part of the plan, carefully selected variety." Skinner smiled. "Perhaps I am a little bit of a collector myself, Mr. Partridge. But I had a practical reason for it. You remember what I said about the different volumes of an encyclopædia on the art of living? All my people were chosen for some special skill or knowledge—except Etia, my Tahitian girl. She joined of her own accord when we were actually on our way here. We had anchored off a secluded part of Tahiti to take on water. Etia swam out during the night and climbed up the anchor chain. Naturally I asked why she did it. I never got more than a hint of the reason. She only had about a dozen words of English at that time. But she impressed me as a person with initiative, who knew her own mind. And it was evident that she had a very poor opinion of men."

"Was not that a disadvantage?"

"Quite the reverse if she was to fit into a community in which there would be no men apart from myself. And she has earned her place by her skill at fishing. Ah, I see by your expression, Mr. Partridge, that you are beginning to appreciate my plan. You will realise how I felt when I first thought of it, walking to the office along the Old Kent Road one Monday morning in the rain. There was a vast amount of detail to be worked out after that, of course. But you have seen something of the result already. We have achieved happiness! My people although young all have considerable experience of life. I felt it was essential. They had to know what they were doing. To put it another way, they had to know when they were well off. And thank goodness they do.

"But I will give you a better idea of the sort of people

they are by telling you the stories of a few of them. Where shall I start? One of the most remarkable concerns my Burmese girl. It is an example of how chance favoured me. I had thought it wise to leave my brig in a secluded creek and was travelling up the Irrawaddy on my own. At a small town, having nothing better to do, I looked in at the local place of justice with the man who acted as my interpreter. A young deer was led into court. The witnesses were on the one hand a girl, and on the other three men.

"The case was as follows. The men had been hunting deer, and to save themselves time and trouble in beating an area of tall reeds and grasses they had set fire to it. One young deer had broken cover, but instead of running towards the guns it had swerved off at right angles, plunged across a stream and rushed panic-stricken into a little bamboo house upon the further bank. The house belonged to the girl witness, Sandana by name. She was a devout Buddhist, and in the moment when the fawn checked at sight of her she had recognised in its eyes the spirit of her only brother who had recently died. She had thrown her arms round it, calmed it, and defied the hunters when they came to take it from her. Realising that they could not kill the deer without first killing her they had gone to court to claim what they considered their rightful prey.

"Sandana on her side doggedly maintained that the fawn was her reincarnated brother. She demonstrated that although it was frightened by the crowded court it was immediately calmed by her touch. I was most impressed by the way she gave her evidence.

"The judge's ruling was a remarkable example of male

129

logic. He disallowed the hunters' claim on the ground that they had failed to prove that the fawn was not Sandana's brother. On the other hand he ruled that she had failed to prove that it was. Therefore the deer would remain the property of the court—in other words of himself."

Skinner paused.

"I bought it from him," he said.

"And gave it back to Sandana?"

"Oh no, Mr. Partridge! I am not a philanthropist. I took it away. And Sandana followed. She had struck me as exactly the type I wanted."

"Are all your stories as dramatic as that?"

"By no means. Most are all too ordinary. In the parts where I was travelling human beings are of little value. I could pick and choose more or less as I liked."

"You talk as if there was still slave trading."

"Of course there is. Do you think our legislation can alter the custom of centuries? Naturally it is covered up. It is difficult to differentiate in polygamous countries between a wife and a slave. But I bought a pair of genuine slaves myself. I came across them in the Straits of Malacca. An Arab merchant who traded somewhere in the Archipelago was on his way back from a pilgrimage to Mecca. He was very proud of himself with his green jacket and his title of Hadji. But once a merchant always a merchant— he could not resist making a profit. He had picked up the twins in Arabia, but they were not as useful as he had hoped, I dare say, because they could not understand a word he said. They only speak English. They were brought up by missionaries, who christened them Faith and Hope."

"There is no Charity?"

"That is what the missionaries were constantly exclaiming, they tell me. You see they come, as well as I can make out, from a Central African tribe where twins are considered unlucky and so are killed at birth. But their mother hid them and supported them until they were old enough to hunt for themselves—like animals in the forest. Somehow the missionaries got hold of them, fed and housed them, educated them as Christians. They are most devout. But the twins tell me that the one thing they could not accept was clothes. They must have been a handful. I dare say the missionaries were not altogether sorry when they went back to the forest."

"They ran away?"

"Into the arms of a slave-raiding party. They were carried across Abyssinia, over the Red Sea to Arabia—where the Hadji Abdulla bought them. And now they are here."

"Don't you, like the missionaries, find them a handful?"

"No, no. It is just a case of treating them the right way, giving them scope. They do all my hunting. They are stronger than most men. They fit in very well. It takes all sorts—Shall we be moving on? You must think me a terrible chatterbox, Mr. Partridge. It is such a pleasure to talk to you, and to show you what I have been able to achieve."

2

Geoffrey walked in silence. He had much to think about. But Skinner soon began talking again.

"One very interesting thing to me is the friendships which have been formed by some of my people. It could never have happened elsewhere, even if the persons concerned had met each other. There would have been prejudices, gossip—all sorts of things to stop it. But here everybody is perfectly natural. They can be themselves and follow their inclinations without fear. I was thinking particularly of those two Africans I have just told you about. Their best friend is my Japanese secretary, Young Bamboo. You smile. It is strange, isn't it?"

"The idea of a secretary in a place like this struck me as a little strange," said Geoffrey.

"Yes, I suppose it is something of an indulgence. I like to have proper records of everything. But I could very well keep them myself. However—how I found her is quite an interesting story.

"I spent a few days in Tokyo as a tourist during the period I have been telling you about. I had not anything particular in mind. I was just looking round. In the smoking room of my hotel one night I overheard some gentlemen discussing Yoshiwara. The general opinion was that it was a well-organised institution which kept vice off the streets. They asked me if I had been there, and when I answered that I had not they advised me to go the next evening to see the festival of inspecting the new flowers.

"I went there in company with an American business man who knew the language. I ought to have been a real tourist! I love to see all the sights. It was an hour's run in a jinrikisha. We reached a huge gate with a weeping willow—the Japanese tree of welcome—on one side, and a police post on the other. The place was surrounded by a wall and a moat, just like a fortress. But inside was a garden city, beautifully laid out. The wide flower-beds which ran down the middle of the streets were full of chrysanthemums of every shade. There were crowds of people in their best clothes, and thousands of paper lanterns and streamers. The sun was shining and you can't imagine the colours even here.

"Then the show started. It was a weird affair. I would not have understood what was happening if my American friend hadn't explained. Each of the Houses had chosen its most beautiful woman to inspect the flowers. They moved very slowly, with their arms held out sideways for balance. Their shoes were lacquered boxes about a foot high, and goodness knows how they walked on them at all. They were each surrounded by a group of servants, some going in front to push the crowd out of the way and one walking on each side of the lady to support her fingertips. They were dressed in the most gorgeous silks, fit for an empress. But beautiful? You couldn't say. You couldn't even guess how old they were. Their faces were so covered with powder and paint that they were just masks. It seemed to me a slow and solemn procession of dummies, all alike.

"As one of these sleep-walking dummies was passing me she caught her shoe in something and went flat on her nose. I never saw such a sudden change in my life. The mask disappeared. She became a silly little girl who had hurt herself. Her face puckered up and she began to cry.

"How the men watching laughed! They rocked and choked and jeered and nearly split themselves with laughter. The girl hid her face in her hands. She couldn't run away because she had turned her ankle falling off those shoes. She put down a hand to touch it—and showed her powered face all smeared with blood from her nose.

"I won't describe any more. Men can be beastly. And old women can be hard as nails. My American friend wanted to get me away. But I made him act as my interpreter. Young Bamboo had appealed to me that moment I saw her become a human being. There was a good deal of hard bargaining and cold legal business during the next few days. But in the end I bought her out for three hundred yen, which was the price her father had sold her for to the House of the Long Blooming Flowers.

"I have never regretted it, Mr. Partridge. She turned out to be really quite pretty when she had washed her face. Her tastes are very simple. She is perfectly happy here. She likes nothing so much as going long walks by herself or with her black friends. She is not a very good secretary, I'm afraid. But she tries hard. And loyal! I verily believe she would give her life for me. All that for thirty pounds. It wasn't a bad bargain after all."

Skinner and Geoffrey completed a circle which brought them back to the freshwater lake.

"Would you care to see the cave?" Skinner asked.

"Yes indeed," said Geoffrey.

They parted the creepers which hung over the entrance —white flowers and green foliage against the yellow ochre of the rock. It was this diversity of colours, and the shadows, Geoffrey realised, which made the cave difficult to see from any distance.

The interior was illuminated by coconut oil lamps— spots of light stretching away and away into the darkness. The flames wavered in moving air which suggested that

134

there were other entrances, or at least vents. The main passage of the cave branched near the entrance. Skinner showed a side-chamber which was his private room. The chief piece of furniture was a great four-poster bed. The posts were stalagmites. A canopy hung from stalactites above.

Going further along the passage they heard voices and laughter, made strange by echoes. A mat curtain hid another chamber.

"The common room," Skinner said, and walked on.

Geoffrey was shown the cellar and store. These were in the lowest part of the great cave where there was an underground pond, in which, said Skinner, there were fish which had no eyes. In another part of the labyrinth were the schoolroom and workroom. In this last there were a number of carved limestone and wooden figures. But none of the artists was to be seen. Geoffrey suddenly felt sure that however long he waited he was unlikely to see any of Skinner's people.

"I am afraid I must be going," he said.

"I suppose you must, or your friends will be looking for you. But do come again," Skinner said.

"May I?"

"I hope you will. I have so much enjoyed our talk. I look forward to many more—when you slip away to chase butterflies! Mr. Partridge, I trust you will excuse me if I do not see you to the pass, but my knee is a little painful after our walk. I will call Silver who will show you the best way."

"When may I come again?" Geoffrey asked.

"Whenever you like."

"I wish a weekday were possible. I would like to see

your people at work. But unfortunately we are kept busy all day long."

"Then come next Sunday. I will meet you at the pass on the southern side. That is more secluded than the other. You know it?"

"I came that way. At what time?"

"Shall we say when the sun is in the south-east? But it matters little. I am free until evening. Ah, here is Silver. You have your butterfly net and bag? Good-bye, Mr. Partridge."

Geoffrey set off with Silver. He was a little alarmed by that intense young woman.

Just before reaching the trees he turned. Skinner had disappeared, but about a dozen girls were standing outside the entrance to the cave. He waved, and they waved back.

A shadow passed over Silver's face. And then she laughed.

She began to talk about the island, its animals and plants. She knew a lot about the butterflies. She did not know their proper names, of course, but she described them so well that he could generally identify them. Walking lightly by his side, treating him in the most natural way, she might have been an English girl, he thought— except for her bare feet and strange garment.

She wanted to know all about his companions. Girls were always inquisitive, Geoffrey knew. He remembered how his sisters used to ask him about his schoolfriends— all sorts of absurd questions. He told Silver anecdotes about Ronald, Harry and Red, and made her laugh.

"What would happen if they came over one day and found you all?"

"They will not do that," Silver said.

"They might, you know," Geoffrey persisted cheerfully. "It is quite possible——"

He broke off. Silver had halted and was facing him. She was no longer an English girl. She was a savage and there was murder in her eyes. When she spoke even her voice had changed.

"Our people love the man who gave them freedom. They hate all other men."

During the remainder of their three mile walk the conversation was spasmodic.

Silver guided Geoffrey to the northern pass, near the cove. There was little more than a shelf between the mountain and the cliff which fell into the sea. He did not enjoy the traverse, especially with Silver watching him.

But when he was on the other side and striding back to camp alone his spirits soared. What an extraordinary adventure! What a story to tell! He began to rehearse it. "There was a clerk in my office who created his own Garden of Eden with a couple of dozen Eves——" Of course it could not be told yet. He would have to wait until they had left the island. But by then it might be even better—he hoped.

3

Red was the only one in camp. He had had a good sleep, and a dream which he described at length. He evidently led a disreputable dream life and it lost nothing of impropriety in the telling. Geoffrey, who had always been amused by his rough form of speech, now felt uncomfortable. He was glad when the other two returned in the boat. Red's vulgarities were always silenced by one of Ronald's stern Presbyterian stares.

Ronald and Harry talked at length of how they had sounded the lagoon. It had proved to be bowl-shaped, except near the mountain shore where they had been unable to reach bottom. Somewhere down there must be the connection with the ocean, as they had already supposed. But their work had been most valuable—in Ronald's view—because they would thenceforward be able, with the chart they had prepared, to dredge the lagoon more systematically, neither missing nor twice fishing any area.

Geoffrey, soon wearying of this shop talk, and being unable to cap it with the story of his own adventure, volunteered to prepare supper.

"Will it be long?" Harry asked. "I want to take the dinghy and do a bit of cave diving."

Ronald objected. "Remember you nearly drowned yourself last time."

"Don't worry. The one thing I have learned so far is to be careful," Harry said.

Before the fishing party left next morning, Geoffrey asked Harry what he was looking for now that they knew the connection with the ocean must be too deep to reach, and what pleasure he could derive from rowing and swimming in the dark.

"It is no more than interestingly dark," Harry said enthusiastically. "There is the light of moon and stars and the phosphorescent water. One dives into a cave and sometimes comes up into a chamber—or under a roof which is below water level, and has to turn back before it is too late. Swimming under water is the most fascinating thing in the world. What scenes for an artist!"

"Let us leave artists alone," Geoffrey said, colouring.

"Why?"

"After what you did to my picture."

"What picture?"

"You know very well. The only one I have painted here—the Sunday before last. It was smeared and smudged."

"It looked like that. But I could only think that you——"

"You mean you did not do it?" Geoffrey asked.

"God, Geoffrey, of course I didn't. I thought you had been trying an experiment in impressionism or whatever they call that excuse for hazy pictures."

At that point Ronald called Harry to the boat.

Geoffrey was housekeeper that day. He managed to save a couple of hours from his labours and used them to build a sort of wigwam for himself at a little distance from the camp site.

When the others returned they laughed at his sudden wish for privacy. None the less, all except Red copied him. Before the end of the week there were three little shelters by the lake shore, each marked in some way by its owner's individuality.

One evening, while Harry was out in the boat and Red sprawled smoking on the quadruple bed of the old sleeping place, Ronald called Geoffrey to his beehive shelter. He had in his hand the pickle jar which contained the pearls. There were many more than when the haul had last been counted. Ronald poured them out on to a blanket. They were of a variety of shapes, shades and sizes. Some were round, more were irregular. The bulk were small as bird-shot, but some were of ten or fifteen grains—the size of peas. A few were larger. They glowed in the light of the lamp which hung from the apex of the shelter.

Ronald asked Geoffrey to explain how they would be valued in the trade.

Geoffrey, who although he had disliked his office work loved pearls for their moonlight beauty, began to talk. He said that shape was of prime importance. The perfect sphere was the ideal. Then came the pear-shaped, the button and the egg-shaped, and last of all the baroque, the odd-shaped. Size was important, but not all-important, for without lustre it was of little worth. Lustre could vary from mirror brightness, through silver down to a mere moonstone sheen. Also to be considered were purity from blemishes, and colour which must be of a shade pleasant to the eye. For pearls were valued for the pleasure they gave. Finally, they were not, ideally, born to live alone but to match others.

Geoffrey fingered the pearls, rolling them into little matching groups—but they were not yet enough to choose from to select a fine necklace. He began to talk about the superstitions which are connected with pearls—how the European and American saying that they bring tears is not found in the mythology of the East, quite the reverse. For many Orientals they are not only lucky but alive. If small pearls are shut up in a close-fitting container with a quantity of rice grains, they will—subject to certain conditions mainly connected with the phases of the moon —grow in size and even breed.

"Never mind about superstitions," Ronald said. "What is this lot worth?"

Geoffrey was loth to give a figure.

"But in less than three months at this rate you will be enabled to live idly and comfortably for the rest of your life," he said.

Ronald did not answer at once. He sat staring at the pearls as if he could see the future in them. Then he began talking of his long-term hopes which he had mentioned to nobody except his own people and Professor Browning. Directly he had made enough money he would put into practice the dream for which he had given up his university career and gone searching the world. He had found the place. Pearling was only a preliminary to bringing out his relations and friends from Corron. Hard-working farmers and fishermen, they would transform the island.

Geoffrey listened with a growing feeling of discomfort. He felt the compliment of being told these things. He heard the emotion in Ronald's voice as he confided that he hoped to bring out a wife and rear a family in these ideal conditions. He often pictured them around him. . . .

While he listened Geoffrey pictured what he had seen the day before, the island already populated. He found nothing to say. He gathered up the pearls and replaced them in the pickle jar.

As a rule he slept soundly, healthily tired as he always was by evening. But that night his thoughts kept him awake. A promise was a promise. But he had at the time been too overcome by surprise to think of the consequences. His loyalty belonged to his leader rather than to Skinner. He ought to tell what he had found beyond the mountain . . . But Ronald at best would be very much disturbed, and needlessly so if the secret could be kept. Besides, he would want to know why he had not been told immediately instead of two days later.

Geoffrey could imagine how Red would behave if he heard about the women. And the restless, wilful Harry too. Quite apart from the trouble which might be caused by spare-time adventures there would be the risk of truancy from work. They were already as short-handed as they could afford to be. If Ronald did not get a sufficient value of pearls his plan would be doomed in any case. If he got the pearls, he could if necessary develop the plan somewhere else. Also there was Skinner's remark about stopping at nothing. Surely it was best to delay the crisis as long as possible—keep the promise.

During the rest of that week there was little time to think of anything except work. Using the chart, they dredged systematically, and daily harvested more oysters than ever before. The pearls had to be transferred from the pickle jar to a pint bottle. On the Friday evening they failed to finish opening the catch before sunset and had to work on by lamplight. This was unsatisfactory, for there was danger of missing pearls.

"In future we will come in an hour earlier," Ronald said.

The others nodded, relieved by this decision, but too tired to talk. They slipped off their clothes and went into the lagoon. They were covered with oyster slime.

Geoffrey only washed himself. He still had to prepare supper.

As he stood by the cooking-fire he sometimes glanced at the others. The moon had risen and he could see them lazing in the water, floating on their backs, now and then splashing. After a while Ronald came out, dressed in his shelter and came to the fire. Then Harry did the same. Then Red, his hair like a carrot-coloured mop.

"Who took my mirror?" he demanded.

They laughed, and his red face became redder.

"One of you must have took it."

Red was really angry.

"Or else it was a bird or a monkey or a cannibal. We ought to have had a good look round before settling down in a place like this. All right, laugh. But whatever it is will take the pearls next."

There was a sound in the bushes. Very likely it was only an animal sound. But Geoffrey had a sudden fear that it was not. He saw Ronald turn in that direction.

"I'm sorry, Red. I borrowed your mirror," Geoffrey said.

"Why?"

"To shave. I couldn't find my own."

"You haven't shaved."

"I had no time."

"Well, where's my mirror?"

"I thought I put it back. We'll find it in the morning." Next morning Red was the last to come to breakfast. He said pointedly that he had been looking for his mirror.

It was Ronald's day as housekeeper, so Geoffrey was in charge of the boat party. He did not have an easy time of it with Red being as difficult as only he knew how. And since for handling the dredge Red's skilled co-operation was essential, the catch was bad. They did not need the extra hour for shell opening.

After the evening bathe Red came slowly from the sleeping place to the cooking fire where the others were waiting for supper.

"I'm sorry, Geoff. I'm sorry, all," he said. "I've found the thing."

"What?"

"My mirror. You'd put it back all right. Only it had slipped under the mattress so to speak."

"All's well then," Geoffrey said.

"Not quite. I sat on it. But I'm glad I found it. My dad gave it me when I started shaving. It's the only thing he ever gave me, bar thrashings."

Geoffrey felt relieved—prematurely. Red was persistent in his repentance. When they were alone after the meal he said, "I'm real sorry I flew off the handle like that."

"It was natural enough," Geoffrey said.

"No. I don't mind admitting when I'm wrong."

Geoffrey was silent.

"What are you doing tomorrow," Red asked.

"Butterflying."

"I'll come with you."

"But you like to sleep on Sunday."

"I want to keep you company, Geoff. Besides, I want to see the other side of the island."

Geoffrey's thoughts once more kept him awake. The position was ridiculous, yet serious. Because of Red's mistaken accusation and his own false confession he was in danger of assisting in what he had lied to prevent—the discovery of Skinner's people.

Sunday was less than ever a day of rest. Ronald intended to build rafts in the cove. His plan was to store the mother-of-pearl shell on those rafts which could be launched on rollers and towed out to the cutter when she returned.

Geoffrey volunteered to help him in carrying wood to

144

the cove. Of necessity Red did the same. So an hour was successfully lost.

Then they climbed to the crest, and Geoffrey turned westward, away from the mountain.

"I thought we were going to the other side," Red complained.

"I want to go right round," said Geoffrey.

"That must be all of twenty miles!"

"We have plenty of time."

They were in the full glare of the sun, and the wind buffeted them. Red began to lag behind.

But when they stopped to eat the lunch which they had brought with them his spirit revived.

"I'll tell you one thing I don't understand," he said in the course of a long and intimate conversation. "I've kept company with quite a few girls. But the one I dream about now's not any of them. How d'you explain that?"

"I can't."

"I thought you would. You've had education. D'you think it means I'm going to meet her?"

"Very likely you will, when you get home."

"Her—in Whitstable!" Red murmured.

Geoffrey contrived to occupy most of the afternoon in reaching a point opposite the camp site. By that time they were both tired and hot. They saw Harry bathing from the boat, exploring the little caves and the creeks which by the hanging vegetation on their banks were hidden from the camp site. They waved to him and he joined them on the shore.

"Will you take us back?" Geoffrey asked.

"But you want to go all round," said Red. "I may look tired, but I keep my promises."

"I *am* tired. I'd rather go back."

They began to row towards the camp.

"I envied you when I saw you on the rim," said Harry. "I love walking, and I have scarcely walked a mile since we arrived."

"You have had plenty of exercise with your cave diving."

"I want more than exercise. I want to explore the whole island," Harry said.

4

That same evening the conversation in camp happened to turn to their ages, and Geoffrey mentioned that the next Thursday would be his birthday.

On Thursday morning Red gave him a box of cheroots and Harry gave him a book. Ronald apologised for having forgotten the occasion. He seemed quite upset. But Geoffrey was thinking about Red's surprising generosity. He had no tobacco to spare, yet gave it away. Geoffrey wondered if he could safely get some from Skinner and make a return gift at a suitable time. But Skinner might have been offended, even made suspicious, by his failure to keep the appointment on the pass.

Ronald was housekeeper that day. In the afternoon, when the others were dredging on the far side of the lake they heard a shot. It startled them by its unexpectedness. It startled the birds too. They rose in clouds from the mountain and from the trees around the shore, calling shrilly.

"That was a gun, not a rifle, wasn't it?" Geoffrey said.

"Getting something for the pot," said Red. "Good luck to him."

"But what does he need a gun for? He told me the cartridges had got to be kept for an emergency."

"That shot came from the other side of the mountain," Red said. "Maybe you need a gun there. What's the matter, Geoff? You look worried. Is there big game on the other side?"

"Not that I noticed," Geoffrey answered, trying to laugh. "But perhaps we ought to go back. Ronald might be in trouble."

"Trouble! We'd get the trouble if we stopped work now. Why shouldn't he go shooting? He's the boss."

"If he had fired from the camp he might have been calling us back. But on the other side of the mountain he could only be hunting," Harry said.

Geoffrey had to give in. They dredged for another hour, and returned to camp at the usual time. Ronald was not there.

The fire had burnt out. But no one liked to suggest again that anything might be wrong. So they sat down and opened the catch.

Still Ronald did not appear. The three men dispersed to look for something which might explain his absence.

"Hi!" Harry shouted from the store. "I can't find the pearls."

"He doesn't keep them there any longer," Geoffrey said. "They are in his hive."

They searched the little shelter. Ronald's personal possessions were neatly arranged. But the bottle of pearls was not there.

By then the sun had set and darkness was growing fast.

"We must go and look for him," Red said.

"I suppose so. But it's no use before the moon rises. When does it rise?" Geoffrey asked.

"In an hour and a half," Harry said. Then, "In mountains, directly you organise a search party for somebody they walk in and laugh at you."

Shortly afterwards Ronald walked into camp. He was carrying a dead turkey.

"Sorry to be late with supper," he said. "Geoffrey, I've a confession I'm ashamed to make. I borrowed your gun and lost it."

His voice was calm, but his manner strange.

"Have you got the pearls?" Geoffrey asked.

"The pearls? I've got a new cache for them. I'll show you."

"What have you been doing?"

Ronald laughed. "I wanted to get something special for your birthday feast. There used to be game beyond the mountain. I had not much time if I was going to cook the thing. I borrowed your gun. And—it vanished."

They got only a brief explanation from him at the time. He was planning for the next day. But this is what had happened to him.

Directly he had finished the chores after the midday meal he had taken the single-barrelled shot-gun, left camp and traversed the mountain by the shelf near the cove. Then he started hunting. But it was some time before he saw any game at all. It seemed to be more scarce, or wild, than formerly. He was glad that he had not trusted to stick or stone for weapons. He was within a mile of the

148

freshwater lake when he came suddenly upon a flock of turkeys which were pecking about in the leaf mould of the forest. Most of them ran into the undergrowth, but a few flew clumsily up into the trees.

An old cock perched on a branch thirty yards away. It worked its neck forward and gobbled at him angrily. He fired—and the whole bird population rose in protest. The noise of the shot and the shrill crying that it caused jarred on one who had never used a modern weapon in this lonely peaceful island which he loved. But he was concerned at something more practical. The shot had been so easy that he had fired carelessly. He had not killed the bird outright. It fell, lay for a moment with its wings spread wide, then scurried away into a thicket.

He went after it. But the bushes were so thick that unless he crawled under their branches he could see nothing. So he lent the gun against a tree and searched for the wounded bird on all fours.

It was some time before he saw it. It was lying quite still, its outstretched neck flat on the ground. He believed it was dead. He crawled to it and reached out a hand. As he touched its feathers it scuttled away.

Wounded though it was it could move more freely under the bushes than he could. It seemed an age before he managed to catch it. And then he did the last act as badly as the rest. There was a lot of flapping and struggling before the sinewy neck was finally broken. Cramped as he was under the bushes, Ronald lay down, hot and exhausted.

Then he crawled out and went to get the gun. He could not find it. Every tree looked like every other tree. He realised that he might well have lost his sense of direction, so he worked systematically across and across the whole area. All that he found—at last—were a few feathers. He felt certain that they marked the place where the bird had fallen. In that case he had recovered his bearings. Still he could not find the gun. It was uncanny. But he forced himself to remain calm and go on searching. He continued until dusk and then returned to camp.

"Let's have something to eat," Ronald said at the end of his first, brief account. "Salt beef or something easy. Tomorrow we go out and clear up the mystery. Then we'll eat the turkey."

Geoffrey said quickly, "There is no need to interrupt the fishing. I will go and find the gun. I'm sure I can."

"You don't even know whereabouts I left it."

"I will if you describe it. And if I fail it does not matter. It's an old gun."

"It is not only the gun. I mean to find whoever took it," Ronald said.

"If anything moved it, it must have been a monkey. I know a monkey could not take it far, but it might drag it among leaves where it got buried."

"That's reasonable," Ronald said. "I had persuaded myself it was something like that before I heard the sound."

"What sound?"

"Just at sunset, as I was giving up—all one's senses seem sharpened at dusk. I heard an axe chopping wood. It was some way off, but unmistakable. No animal could imitate that."

"You told us that you had explored every square yard of the island," Harry said.

"When I was here before it was uninhabited. But that is over two years ago. People could have come since.

What do you think, Red? You're a down-to-earth fellow."

"Sounds like there's someone," Red answered. "Better take rifles. It might be cannibals."

"Red Mallett scared!" Ronald said, laughing.

"Should be. I'm the tastiest. But look at Geoff—white as a fish's belly."

He would have to prevent the search. He would have to tell. But it was hard to find the opportunity. No one must know except Ronald, and they were all together until they went to their beds. He followed Ronald to his shelter but was told to go off to his own and get some sleep.

A little before dawn Geoffrey heard sounds—birds waking suddenly, startled by something. He crept out of his shelter. If they were being watched, if he could get in touch with the watchers, he might send a message to Skinner to hide in the cave.

But he saw no one—until Ronald appeared. He would have to tell. But before he could do so Harry joined them, then Red. They prepared some breakfast.

Ronald said, "I'd better show you where I put the pearls. Just in case——" He led the way towards his shelter.

"I'll follow in a moment," Geoffrey said.

He went to the store as if to check the rifles. He waited until the others were leaving Ronald, then he joined him.

Ronald was standing beside a tree at the water's edge. The tree tilted over the lagoon. On the landward side its roots had been partly pulled out of the ground, forming a sort of cage. The bottle of pearls was in this cage, covered with dead leaves.

"I don't know what made me think of hiding them," Ronald said. "Some instinct, I suppose. There have been

151

several strange incidents since we arrived, if you come to think of it."

"Yes," Geoffrey said. "Ronald, there are people on the island."

Ronald looked at him keenly.

"You saw signs of them when you were after butterflies?"

"I saw them."

Geoffrey told his story. It was very far from being the good joke—"There was a clerk in my office"—as he had originally rehearsed it. He felt awkward and ashamed. But he was grateful to Ronald for letting him speak without interruption, and for what he said when the story came lamely to its end.

"I can see you got yourself into a cleft stick. But the only real difference is that if you had told me at once we could have settled this thing sooner."

"What are you going to do?" Geoffrey asked.

"You and I will go and deal with this man Skinner. He must take his harem somewhere else."

"But how?"

"As he came. He can't surely have marooned himself with that crowd. He has got to clear out. This is my island. No one and nothing is going to interrupt my plan."

"What about Harry and Red?" Geoffrey asked.

"They had better know nothing. You were right about that. One minute while I talk to them. Then we'll go and settle with this chief clerk of yours."

5

"Why did he change his mind?" Harry said, looking after the retreating pair as they disappeared among the trees.

"You heard him," Red said, making himself comfortable against a tree. "If there are savages we can't leave the camp unguarded."

Harry continued to wander restlessly about, hands in pockets, a thoughtful frown on his face.

At last he halted beside Red.

"I'm going to make sure there is no one spying on us."

"How are you going to do that?"

"Simply. Those two went by the northern pass. I'll row across the lake and have a look at the southern one."

"What about me?"

"You stay here. I'll hardly go out of sight."

"What if I'm attacked?"

"You'll not be attacked. Don't be frightened."

"I'm not frightened. Life isn't all that worth living."

"Cheer up, Red. I'll soon be back."

Red watched Harry launch the boat and row energetically towards the southern side. The water was as brilliant as a mirror under the sun. He began to blink, on each occasion keeping his eyes shut for a longer period. Then his body drooped. After a little while he was lying flat.

Some forty minutes later Harry heard a shot. It had been fired from beyond the mountain. He could not be certain whether it had been fired from a rifle or a gun. If a gun it meant that the other two had found the first thing they were looking for. If a rifle—he could not guess the explanation. But they were two men, both armed. He was less concerned for them than about Red's possible reaction. Red might do anything. He ran to the boat and rowed back to camp as hard as he could.

He found Red sitting with his back against a tree trunk, just as he had left him.

"You look hot," Red said.

"Didn't you hear that shot?" Harry asked.

"There hasn't been no shooting."

"What have you been doing, Mr. Sentry?"

"Harry, I have been conversing with the most beautiful girl," Red said impressively.

"You've been dreaming."

"Harry, I saw her as clear as I see you. Call that dreaming! She had on a sort of dressing-gown and her hair was all piled up shiny and black—just like a picture in the woman's perrukier at Chatham I once saw . . . Sweet little face. Shy. And her shape! I could make it out all right." Red's short-fingered hands drew an outline in the air. "She wanted to run away. But I soothed her. And in no time we were great friends. Leastwise I thought we were. Then all of a sudden she slapped my face. Made quite a bang it did."

Harry did not smile. He looked down at Red thoughtfully.

"Just for a moment I nearly believed it," he said.

"I nearly believe it myself, still. Cor!"

"Red, what would you do if you really saw a woman?"

"Do? I'll tell you what I wouldn't do. I wouldn't tell you about it."

6

"We don't need these weapons," Geoffrey said.

"We must leave the camp with them," said Ronald. "What would the others think if I say I'm afraid of an attack on the camp, and we go unarmed?"

He climbed rapidly to the rim. Then came the traverse which made Geoffrey as giddy as before. Beyond, Ronald strode off through the forest at a tremendous pace. He knew where the cave was. Geoffrey had some difficulty in keeping up.

"We can leave the rifles now," he said.

"Leave them? I lost a gun yesterday," Ronald answered.

Geoffrey glanced at his face and saw that it was set and stern. His heart began to sink.

He said, "We can hide them in some easily identifiable place. After all, what do we want them for?"

Ronald did not even glance at him. Striding on he answered, "Who knows what he might not try, a man like that."

The farther they went, the more embarrassed Geoffrey felt. Ronald had taken the story so well. His reaction was always inclined to be slow, but unfortunately there was nothing half-hearted about it when it set in. One could not entirely blame him in this case. It was an extraordinary situation to be faced with all of a sudden. Still, something had got to be done to calm him down.

Geoffrey said, "I gave you only a very sketchy picture

of Skinner. He is really a very nice chap. He used to be extremely kind and helpful to me in the office. Of course he is a little odd——"

"Don't shield the man," Ronald interrupted. "It would be bad enough to have anyone trespassing on my island. But with a whole crowd of women!"

Geoffrey kept silent for another half-mile or more. Ronald, for all his education, in spite of his wide travels, was still at heart the son of a little Highland village where the minister fulminated every Sabbath against the sins of the flesh. In a crisis of emotion this was the side of him which came to the surface. But he had got to be restrained —and quickly. They were, Geoffrey thought, within a mile of the cave.

He laid a hand on Ronald's arm.

"It is no use starting a quarrel before you even meet. You will find him straightforward and honest, I promise you, if you treat him the right way. But we will only put ourselves in the wrong if we burst in on him like a couple of moss troopers."

Ronald suddenly halted. "Very well, I'll warn him," he said.

He unslung his rifle and fired it into the air.

It seemed to Geoffrey that he had never heard so loud an explosion. It echoed from the mountain and a million birds rose screaming. Then, little by little, silence returned. Absolute silence.

Ronald ejected the used cartridge case and worked another into the breech. Then, the rifle balanced in his hands, he leaned his back against a tree.

Geoffrey stood beside him, continually turning his head from side to side. But he saw nothing except trees with flowering creepers twisting up their stems and hanging from their branches. There was no sound at all.

All of a sudden Silver was standing in front of them. They had not seen her approach, but the red petals of a creeper behind her were still slowly falling. She wore the same plain sarong as on the Sunday before. She was bare-footed and her bare arms hung by her sides. Her large dark eyes in her rather pale face looked at the two armed men with interest, but without surprise.

Geoffrey burst out, "This is our leader, Ronald Mackin-tosh. He has got to see Mr. Skinner at once on most important business."

"Oh yes," said Silver. "Will you come this way?"

7

They left the forest, traversed the glades of fruit trees and flowering bushes and reached the green bowl.

Skinner was sitting under the great tree outside the cave. Silver, who had gone on in front, was talking to him. There was no one else in sight. He rose and came forward a few paces to meet the two men.

"Mr. Mackintosh? How do you do? Good morning, Mr. Partridge," he said.

Geoffrey looked from him to Ronald. They were a strongly contrasting pair—Ronald in European clothes, tall and bearded, showing determined self-assurance as a dog shows its hackles, Skinner dressed only in sandals and a white sarong, clean shaven and a full head shorter. There was nothing hostile nor even unfriendly in Skinner's attitude. Nor was there any hint of either alarm or servility. With his slight bow and his gestured invitation that they should come into the shade he was a host receiving guests, perhaps business acquaintances, in his own home.

Ronald stood his ground.

"You will have to leave the island," he said. His tone was not actually rude, but it was very firm. He was stating a fact.

Skinner, still in the same welcoming attitude, looked at him unblinkingly for perhaps a quarter of a minute.

"Let us discuss it, Mr. Mackintosh," he said.

"There is nothing to discuss," said Ronald.

Silver quickly turned her head and looked at th green-curtained mouth of the cave. Geoffrey saw the creepers move.

Skinner said easily, "Excuse me, there are one or two strictly practical questions which do need discussing. And we might as well be comfortable. Please sit down. Let me take your rifle."

Ronald after a slight hesitation handed him the weapon. Skinner hung it, and Geoffrey's, on a branch of the tree. The three men sat down. Silver withdrew into the cave.

"You feel that I should leave the island?" Skinner said.

Ronald looked at him in silence for a moment. Then he said slowly, "Yes, that is so. It may sound hard. But I must insist upon it. There is no room for two communities here—two such different communities. And this island is mine."

"Have you considered, sir, how I and my people might go?" Skinner asked.

"I presume you have a supply ship."

"I had a ship, Mr. Mackintosh. But before we had quite finished unloading she slipped away. I have no proof, but it seemed done by design, not accident. The native crew had for some time been worried and nervous about the voyage, about my whole venture. And it was clear that they were made uneasy by this island. The fact that they could not reach bottom with an anchor even close to the shore appeared supernatural to men of the shallow seas. The blow-holes alarmed them. I mention these details to show you that even if my ship is still afloat it is beyond the bounds of reasonable possibility that she should return."

Ronald said, "You are telling me, in fact, that you have no link whatever with the outside world?"

"That is so. But I promise you one thing now, Mr. Mackintosh. If you convince me that I have no right to be here I will take myself off, if necessary in a canoe or a raft."

Ronald moved his long legs restlessly. Skinner sat—it seemed with comfort—in the native attitude. But Ronald and Geoffrey doubled their legs up to the side, leaning first on one arm then the other.

"We have no independent judge," Skinner went on. "But I believe that you will play fair and accept the ruling of logic. On what do you base your claim to the island?"

"Briefly—let us be brief—on prior occupation."

"You consider that a sufficient claim?"

"In the circumstances—yes, I do."

"When did you arrive in the island?"

"Three years ago. On that occasion I was here for eleven months."

"I was here before that, Mr. Mackintosh," Skinner said.

Ronald coloured slightly. He said:

"In his report to me this morning Mr. Partridge mentioned that you told him you had been here for only a year."

He glanced at Geoffrey, who nodded. He went on. "He also told me that you had been actively working out your —your paradise for two and a half years. Even so, I was on the island before you began this active preparation— whatever that may mean."

Skinner, for the first time, smiled.

"It meant a great deal of travelling, of patient negotiation, of careful and occasionally dangerous work. But I must not digress to tell you about that now. When I mentioned to Mr. Partridge that I had been here for a year I meant on this occasion, with my people. I first visited this island twenty-seven years ago."

Geoffrey opened his mouth with surprise. But Ronald's expression did not change.

"We had better define what we each mean by a visit— a chance glimpse or something more," he said. "I explored the island thoroughly, lived on its produce——"

"I am sure you were struck by the variety and profusion of that produce," Skinner said. "The delicious fruits, for example. Tell me, did you pause to consider how they came to be here?"

Ronald impatiently moved his legs.

"I have been told by scientific men that birds are the chief carriers of seeds," he said.

"Yes. That probably accounts for most of the vegetation here. But not all. For instance, can you imagine a bird carrying a coconut? Forgive me for stressing this point, Mr. Mackintosh, but how could they have come? They could not have drifted ashore as they do on most desert islands, for there is no beach. This is not an atoll. The explanation is that they were brought by me. I also brought and planted orange, banana, bread-fruit trees, guavas, pineapples, sugar cane, maize, rice and many other things besides. Therein lies my definition of a visit."

"You appear to have been remarkably well-equipped," Ronald said.

"I can understand your scepticism, Mr. Mackintosh. Let me explain. I was travelling for my firm—visiting places where we already had interests, to see how our agents were getting on and to assist them in any practical way. Also I was surveying undeveloped or uninhabited localities which might be worth developing. In those early days it was my firm's policy to make our more isolated concessions as self-supporting as possible. For instance, a bêche-de-mer fishery, or a copra factory, might have its own farm. That helped to ease the problem of supply. So on our schooner we carried a quantity of seeds and rooted cuttings. When, in the course of an extensive tour, I landed on this island I fell in love with it—as I believe you did also, Mr. Mackintosh. It was not for me to decide that it should be developed. My stated task was only to write a report on it—which I did. But so impressed was I by the potentialities of the island that—entirely on my own responsibility—I decided to take time by the forelock, so to speak. I turned a few of the sailors into horticulturists, and while the schooner lay off we planted from dawn till sunset—and half the night as well since there was a moon."

Ronald was silent. Skinner went on.

"If you cut down one of the original fruit trees—which I trust you will not—you would be able to count twenty-seven annual rings. That is if what I was told as a child is true, of course. Another piece of evidence occurs to me. I dare say your party were struck by the similarity of the bird you shot yesterday with a farm-yard turkey. It was a farm-yard turkey, the descendant of some birds we had on the schooner. They had been intended for the Christmas tables of our agents in various out-of-the-way places. But—I was feeling so happy. It seemed to me about time that turkeys had a happy Christmas too . . . And the monkeys—Young Mr. Pinkerton, who was not on board during this part of the trip, had previously collected several monkeys as presents for his friends at home. But when the weather was fair they were up to all sorts of mischief, a great trouble to the crew. And when it was rough they were so horribly seasick. So—largely to pacify the crew, I admit—I took it upon myself to put them ashore."

"Are you going to tell me that you imported the tortoises as well?" Ronald asked.

"No, Mr. Mackintosh. Only God, and perhaps Father Noah, know why they are on this island. But apart from them, and the birds, I am responsible for all the animal population, as I am for most of the useful trees and plants. So you will understand my proprietary feeling."

Ronald sat thinking for a little while. Then he said, "Your firm was Pinkerton and Powell, I believe. Mr. Pinkerton invested in my expedition. But he never mentioned that one employee of his had been here."

"In business, Mr. Mackintosh, one does not disclose

information unnecessarily. Young Mr. Pinkerton generally adopted my recommendations as his own and forwarded them as such to the chairman, his father. Only in the case of this island did he ignore my advice. It seems likely that after all these years he has had second thoughts."

"You mentioned the pearls in your report?" Geoffrey asked.

"Oh yes."

"And yet Pinkerton was against the island?"

"There were not so many oysters in those days," Skinner said. "Or else they had been buried in sand by the earthquake."

"What earthquake?"

"I believe there had been a violent one not very long before I arrived. That little cove one lands in was formed then, I think. The broken rocks were quite unweathered. And there was a slight tremor while I was here. Nothing serious. It was just as if one were dizzy for a moment. But I mentioned it in my report. Mr. Pinkerton was put off by that. And by the difficulties of communications. And the fact that the only possible pearling area was the lagoon which is quite small——"

"The pearls are the only things I am interested in," Ronald said. "You don't claim them?"

"No, no. You are welcome to them while you are here, Mr. Mackintosh. Before you came my people used occasionally to dive for them on Sundays. But it was only a pastime. We are too busy for that sort of thing. There is so much to do."

Ronald and Geoffrey remained silent. Skinner, clasping his knees, continued in a reminiscent tone.

"When young Mr. Pinkerton turned down my recommendations for this island I believed myself the most disappointed young man in the world. I did not regret the hard work I had given. A junior employee must be prepared for that. But I had given my heart as well. It was little consolation that Mr. Pinkerton congratulated me on all my other reports and gave me a bonus. But to be criticised for "unauthorised expenditure on a virtually inaccessible and valueless island"—That is how he described it. I was tempted to go out and get drunk. Instead I spent my bonus on tickets for a sweepstake—and lost it all.

"Well, we returned to England where old Mr. Pinkerton confirmed all his son's decisions. I was told to file my report on this island under Rejected Propositions.

"Gradually the revelation dawned on me. Fate had not been unkind. It had only moved in a mysterious way. The island had been preserved—*for me*. It was up to me to work for it. But how? I had learned the value of money —and I had no capital at all. If I told you my salary at the time it would make you smile. But that oriental sweepstake was associated in my mind with the providential turning down of my report and I was convinced that my way lay in subscribing to it regularly.

"I began walking to and from the office. I reduced my meals. I neither smoked nor drank. I could not prevent myself from marrying. Mine is not a monkish nature. But for twenty-five years I continued to save enough to buy sweepstake tickets and to educate myself by reading. I walked, I have calculated, one hundred and five thousand miles—equivalent to four times round the world. While walking I thought out the details of the ideal state which

164

I am now developing. You will understand that I feel strongly about it."

"Yes, I understand," Ronald said slowly. "I have lived on dreams—more dreams than food sometimes—to find this island. I have been round and round the world. Now I am here, and my dreams have turned to plans. I feel strongly——"

"So strongly that you feel justified in demanding that I leave the island, by canoe or raft?"

Ronald could not prevent himself from smiling. "No, I do not feel justified in doing that," he said.

"Then the choice is simple. We will have no communication with the outside world for the next two months or more. Meanwhile, therefore, we must either fight to the death or live in peace."

"I have no wish to fight—particularly with women," Ronald said.

"Yet you came armed, Mr. Mackintosh."

"Because you have a gun of ours."

"What is that?"

"The gun with which I shot the turkey. One of your people took it."

"No," Skinner said. "You must be mistaken."

Ronald and Geoffrey looked at him, then at each other.

Skinner went on, "I sincerely believe that you do not consider the use of force. For so short a period we can surely live segregated and in peace."

"Certainly. I do not want to be interrupted in my work any more than I expect you do."

"That is exactly what I had hoped to hear," said Skinner with a sudden smile. "We will not interrupt or interfere with each other in any way."

"Are you sure—Excuse the question, Mr. Skinner, but it is as well to be frank. I will answer for my party as long as yours keep bounds. Are you sure that you can keep a tight enough rein on all of them?"

"Quite sure. I will not trouble you with the reasons, which are personal to them and to me. But I will give you proof. As soon as you arrived I told them that they must give up their spare time habit of bathing in the lagoon. They have obeyed implicitly. I shall repeat what I said, still more strongly. You will excuse me if I paint your characters a little black. But I promise you that you will not be troubled. Now may I ask a question? Can you assure me that you will leave the island directly your ship returns?"

"If I have gathered a sufficient number and value of pearls."

"You will have gathered all the pearls, Mr. Mackintosh. At your present rate of work—we have observed you— you will have entirely fished out the lagoon in two months from now."

"That is what I am beginning to think."

"In that case shall we shake hands on our bargain to leave each other alone during these two or three months of your stay?"

"I would like to," Ronald answered. "But there is something else which I have to tell you. I shall be going, as I said. But I intend to come back."

"At once?"

"No. Not before a year, probably longer. But I intend to return with some of my own people."

Sitting cross-legged, his head slightly on one side, Skinner considered this.

"Mr. Mackintosh. I blamed myself for allowing you to land," he said. "As it has turned out, no harm was done. We have talked together openly and come to an understanding. But once you go I do not believe that I and my people would allow another landing. However, that is a long way off. If necessary we can talk again before you leave. Now, let us shake hands on what we have decided for the immediate future."

Chapter Six

I

As they started back towards their camp, Ronald appeared in so much better humour than on the outward journey that Geoffrey said to him:

"You got on very well with Skinner. Did you like him?"

"He is disarming," Ronald said. He strode on a few paces and suddenly burst out, "But how can one like a man who has no morals at all?"

"You and he will never see eye to eye there! But at least he is transparently sincere."

"You think so?" Ronald asked.

"What makes you doubt it?"

"The gun for one thing. He pretended to know nothing about it. Surely he must, for surely it was taken. Then he said his people obeyed his order not to bathe in the lagoon. But he knew in detail about our dredging. Have you not had the feeling of being watched from close at hand? And that monster or bevy of mermaids we hunted one night— what logical explanation is there except that some of his women were fooling about in the water?"

"I know he is a great believer in liberty," Geoffrey said soothingly. "But whatever may or may not have happened in the past I am quite sure that he will keep all the conditions of the peace."

"Oh yes, he'll do that—for his own sake. He will hold his hussies in check."

They walked on in silence for a while. Then Ronald asked violently, "How many wives has he?"

"That first day I saw about a dozen women. But I don't know if that is all there are, and what their position is."

"It is perfectly disgusting in any case," Ronald said. "They are not going to remain on this island. I made that clear enough, didn't I? I told him at the start that there was no room for two communities, and I told him at the end that I will be bringing my own people."

"You made everything clear," Geoffrey said, looking away. With the burden of secrecy off his mind he felt light-hearted, and he was amused that Ronald's moral outburst had only come when he was removed from the influence of Skinner's gentle charm. "You and Skinner were perfectly open with each other," he went on. "But tell me, how will you actually remove him and his people?"

"Don't you bother about that," Ronald said.

Geoffrey thought it best to change the subject.

"What are you going to say to Red and Harry?" he asked.

"This is a case where the proper end is clear and any means are justified in obtaining it," Ronald said. "Those two must be kept away from the Toe. If I ordered them not to go there they might be tempted to find out why. So we are going to lie to them, and lie well. Firstly, there are no human beings there. Secondly, the other half of the island is not worth the long walk. Fortunately you were scratched and had nothing good to say of the Toe when

169

you came back that first time. We will just improve on that impression."

"What about the axe blows you said you heard yesterday, and the gun?"

"They will be glad enough to think that I can be mistaken and lose things," Ronald said, and smiled at last.

Geoffrey said doubtfully, "Harry has an inquisitive mind and Red is no fool."

Ronald chuckled.

"I will make sure there is no wandering by working you all so hard that the Sabbath day is spent in rest as it was meant to be."

Back in camp, Ronald described their expedition as he had said he would. They had searched as thoroughly as was possible in four hours. If there had been any human beings about they would certainly have come on signs of them, but there was none. The sound he had thought was axe blows must have been made by some sort of woodpecking bird. As for the gun, how he had lost it was still unsolved. But he had fired a rifle shot in about the same part of the forest—it was impossible to locate the exact spot—and he and Geoffrey had waited in hiding, but had seen nothing.

Geoffrey listened to this unlikely tale, closely watching the faces of Harry and Red. He saw no sign of incredulity. But after all, he realised, that was not surprising. He himself would never have imagined that Ronald could speak anything except the strictest truth. And the way he told his lies—with stern determination—carried conviction and silenced questions.

"Have you anything to report?" he asked when he had said all that he felt had to be said.

"Nothing," Harry answered. "Everything has been as quiet as the grave—except for Red and me keeping each other company with talk."

In the afternoon they went dredging—except Red who was housekeeper.

The evening oyster opening, although there was less than the usual quantity of shell, was unusually productive. Also it was exciting. First one of them found a valuable pearl, then another found a better, or one which he claimed was better. The sporting competition grew. Their laughter rang against the shrill crying of the birds. They were in high spirits.

For supper Red gave them a large fish which he had caught on a fixed line set in the deepest part of the lagoon, close to the mountain. They had not had a fish of that sort before and it was very good.

"Of course you know more about fishing than any of us," Ronald said. "In future you will be in sole charge of the net and lines."

"Takes time, a line. A net takes longer. You got to find out where the fish lie."

"Harry will help you. With all the diving he has done he must know every fish by sight."

It was one of the most cheerful evenings they had had. Geoffrey almost forgot what he had felt at midday, a sense of division in the party. Then it had seemed to him that they were divided into two pairs, much as the ship's company had been divided into crew and land party directly the island was sighted.

In fact, as the time which followed showed, there

existed a certain degree of division. But the ship's company simile did not hold. Then some had been going to fish for pearls and the rest to do something quite different. Now they all fished for pearls, cleaned the shell, carried it to the cove and stacked it there—worked together harder than ever. They were still a team, even if two of them knew something which they kept from the other two.

They dredged the lagoon, following a geometrical plan, and it soon became evident that they would cover the whole fishing area before the cutter returned. Still Ronald drove them hard. "Let us get the job done. Then nothing will matter," was his point of view.

After the first month there were too many pearls to go into the bottle. They were transferred to a stone demijohn which had contained rum. After two months this was already half full. Admittedly the bulk was of small pearls. But Geoffrey estimated that the total value would amply cover Ronald's migration plan, and also pay off with interest his indebtedness to Pinkerton and Powell and to Lady Warden.

Still Ronald kept up the pressure.

"We might as well make sure. There will be the bigger dividend for everyone," he said. "We have nothing better to do."

2

Hundreds of insects paid with their lives for Geoffrey's secret relaxation. He used to set off every Sunday morning with all the paraphernalia of butterfly net, killing-bottle and collector's field box. When he returned in the evening there were plenty of specimens in the box. In camp he used to murmur impressive Latin names over them. But in fact not very many of them were really worth keeping, and he had not spent many of his hours of absence in collecting. But he had to bring something back to substantiate what he said he had been doing.

What he had actually been doing for most of the time was talking with Skinner. They used to meet in a place which Skinner called the Club. It was a shelf on the outside of the island's rim, on the north coast near the cave— a pleasant place shaded by an overhanging rock and padded with ferns and mosses. There they would sit talking in the leisurely manner of friends, lazily looking at the restless ocean and sipping coconut punch.

Skinner used to arrive with an air of mild mischief, like a family man who has slipped away from the cares of domesticity for a quiet drink with a crony. He placed the basket and gourd he had brought in a cool spot under the ferns and settled down to fill his pipe. He often said how much he enjoyed these meetings. Geoffrey enjoyed them too. It was a delightful way of spending Sunday after a hard week, and Skinner was always worth listening to. But he would have preferred to meet in the green bowl outside the cave where he had first seen the women.

This, however, was never suggested. Nor did Skinner ever talk with the same freedom about his people as he had in the excitement of their first meeting. Geoffrey observed the unwritten laws of club life and curbed his inquisitiveness. Skinner was even more discreet. But they sometimes played an unacknowledged game, each trying to draw out the other unobtrusively.

It was man talk that Skinner wanted—about farming, of which Geoffrey knew little and cared less, about books which he had read or wished that he had read (he had lost most of his library during the landing), about countries which they had both visited and occasionally about life in England as opposed to life on the island.

"Of course one has not got everything here," Skinner said. "That is one reason why I enjoy our talks so much. But I learned a long time ago that one must be prepared to pay for everything. And—apart from our talks—the little lacks and discomforts seem to me a very small price for health, a perfect climate and peace to get on with the things that interest one."

"You have your people," Geoffrey said.

"Yes, we are self-contained."

"Solomon," said Geoffrey, looking out to sea, "the wisest man in the world, had seven hundred wives."

The flicker of a smile passed over Skinner's face.

"To me, Mr. Partridge, such figures are meaningless," he said. "Twenty-one seemed to me a practical number— twenty actually, since Etia was outside my calculations. They do work very well. You have seen the fields they have cleared and cultivated . . ."

And so they were back to farming. On another occasion Skinner spoke about Ronald—in the most complimentary terms. "He has kept our bargain scrupulously," he said. "I would like to show something of my appreciation. Silver has inherited her mother's wonderful gift as a pearl surgeon. Before you came one of the girls, diving for fun, brought home a sizeable pearl which was full of blemishes. Silver cleaned it up so successfully that if I were still interested in commerce—well, I would have even more reason to call her a jewel. Do you think Mr. Mackintosh would be interested? If he cared to bring along any

174

imperfect pearls, Silver would almost certainly be able to improve their value."

When Geoffrey told Ronald about Skinner's offer to have his pearl crop improved by doctoring, he made no comment. A few evenings later when the four men were opening the day's catch Red gave a triumphant shout and held out on the palm of his hand a pearl as large as a pickled onion.

"The champion of champions! What's it worth, Geoff?"

Geoffrey examined it. The big pearl was less symmetrical than a pickled onion, but it had much the same dirty yellow colour.

"Quite a lot. But not as much as many smaller pearls that we have already," he said.

Red protested hotly. He said that Geoffrey was jealous because he had not found it himself. It was a magnificent pearl.

"Would you want to wear it if you were a beautiful woman?" Geoffrey asked.

They laughed, looking at Red who was naked and covered with oyster slime.

But as they worked on Ronald asked seriously whether the pearl had not a considerable rarity value.

"Yes, of course. But not very much else, I'm afraid," Geoffrey said. "I am talking from the point of view of Pinkerton and Powell to whom I suppose you will have to offer it. They are not interested in oddities and one can't call this beautiful. But if they refuse it, and if you could find a gambler, you might get hundreds of pounds."

"A gambler?"

"Who would skin it like an onion on the chance that there was something better inside."

"Would he not spoil it, hacking it about?"

"As likely as not. And more likely than not there is nothing better inside. It would just get smaller and smaller as each layer was peeled off, or be spoiled altogether. That is why the gambler would be hard to find."

At that stage the conversation was changed by the behaviour of one of the gulls. It had gorged itself until it could not swallow any more, or even fly away. It stood with ruffled feathers, staring at the ever growing pile of delicious food, opening and closing its beak and looking utterly miserable.

When the work was done the men had their swim, then supper. After that Harry and Red went off fish spearing. Red had taken his responsibility as chief fisherman very seriously, and Harry had persuaded him to add to what he could get on a line or in the net by trying his hand at spearing by torch light from the dinghy. They both evidently enjoyed the sport and sometimes brought back quite good catches.

On this particular evening Ronald and Geoffrey sat watching the guttering light as it moved along the further shore and sometimes disappeared into a cave or inlet, leaving only a faint reflected gleam upon the water.

"How is this pearl doctoring done?" Ronald suddenly asked.

"No practitioner will ever tell you," Geoffrey answered. "It is a secret art, and a very rare one. I have only seen two operations. One was by a Singalese and the other by a Chinaman. It was the most delicate surgery combined with magic. Each had his own method, and his own primitive tools. But each seemed able to see inside the pearl, to know where to scrape and how far he could go."

"What do you mean by magic?"

"I suppose it is knack—part born gift, part experience."

"Do you believe this woman Silver has the knack?"

"I only have Skinner's word for it. But he is a pretty good judge. Why don't you try her? We could pick out a few suitable pearls."

"Very well. If that is what you suggest. You could handle the whole thing, couldn't you?"

"It would be better if you came yourself. They are your pearls."

Eventually a meeting was arranged one Sunday afternoon at a place in the forest near to the northern pass. Geoffrey accompanied his leader. Skinner came with Silver. ('It might have been a duel,' Geoffrey thought). Silver carefully examined the pearls which Ronald had brought. She divided them into two groups, one of which she handed back to Ronald.

"Why?" he asked.

"Because they cannot be improved," she said definitely. "Which of these others do you wish me to treat first?"

Ronald chose a baroque. She began scraping, using a small knife blade and continually turning the pearl. She worked so fast that it was impossible even from close at hand to see exactly what she was doing. But at frequent intervals she paused, examined the pearl, showed it to Ronald and asked whether she should continue. He nodded, and she went on—while an infinitely fine snow fell from the shrinking pearl.

She stopped finally of her own accord. It was not worth going any further, she said. She polished the pearl with

177

soft leather, then energetically between her palms and handed it to Ronald. It was of about half its original size, but of considerably better shape and with a purer colour.

Ronald put it away with evident relief. Throughout he had watched as closely as if a loved relation were being operated on. But he thanked the surgeon warmly and allowed her to treat a more valuable pearl. In due course, at the price of a third of the pearl's bulk, she removed an ugly black spot.

Ronald was in excellent spirits as they walked to the camp some hours later.

"She is a straightforward lass," he said. "No nonsense about her."

He was anxious, if it could safely be achieved, to arrange other meetings when more of the pearls might be attended to.

As it turned out, there was no difficulty at all. Harry and Red were content to spend their Sundays swimming or rowing on the lagoon and showed little or no interest in what their companions did. But only on one other occasion was Geoffrey present at a pearl skinning. That was when Red's monster was operated on.

To begin with he was even more interested in Ronald's behaviour than in the work. Ronald sat watching with nervous intentness, biting his lip, as the big pearl shrank and shrank under Silver's nimble fingers—and yet showed nothing better underneath.

"Shall I go on?" she asked half a dozen times.

"Yes," he said—each time with less conviction.

Suddenly a crack appeared. Ronald drew in his breath as if he had been physically hurt. Geoffrey looked as closely as he could—and was anxious. There is nothing

178

much one can do with a cracked pearl. The only hope, it seemed to him, was that the crack did not go deep. Then it might possibly be closed.

Silver had paused. Moving her head from side to side as she examined the pearl her hair came down like a curtain. But soon the movement of her arms showed that she had started working again.

"What are you doing?" Ronald asked sharply.

Silver did not answer, but with a sudden toss of the head she threw back her hair.

Her knife blade was moving rapidly to and fro along the line of the crack. She was opening the wound. Something bright was just visible beneath, like the sun seen through a narrow rent in a cloudbank. No one spoke. They were all as tense as violin strings which are being tightened, tightened. Something must break . . .

The pearl broke. It split right open. And inside it lay a perfect pearl—spherical, flawless, glowing with beauty.

3

The mountain attracted any rain clouds which might be floating about in the area. Showers—varying from a few enormous drops to a brief and concentrated downpour— were fairly frequent. They were always welcome. They freshened the air, revived the greenery and kept the springs flowing. But the storm on the night of the 3rd of March was another thing altogether.

The day was oppressive, increasingly so as the hours dragged by. There was no breeze at all even in the middle of the lagoon. Every action was an effort and every little thing which went wrong jarred upon the nerves. The men quarrelled over trifles as they had never done before. The atmosphere was literally charged, for if one of them ran his fingers through his hair it crackled.

Ronald blamed himself for not bringing a barometer from the cutter.

"What's the good of a barometer," Red asked. "Anybody can tell a storm's coming."

Yet the sky was perfectly clear.

They dredged until the usual hour, then returned to camp and began opening the shells, after taking the unusual precaution of pulling the boat up high and dry and turning her upside down.

The sun sank below the rim of the island. This was always a welcome moment, for after spending the whole day on the unsheltered lagoon they were at last in shadow, and yet there remained plenty of light to work by, for sunset would not come for another half-hour.

But on this evening it almost immediately and quite suddenly became night. The whole sky darkened and the stars leaped out. The birds, taken unawares, set up a tremendous crying and chattering as they feverishly sought their roosting places. Those which had been feeding on the oysters streaked away as if things invisible to men were attacking them.

Yet all the sky which could be seen was perfectly clear.

"We'll leave these," Ronald said, referring to the unopened oysters. "Let's make certain everything is snug—and get a good supper inside us."

He was as calm before this phenomenon of nature as Geoffrey had seen him put off balance by things emotional. Geoffrey himself had been considerably affected by the

180

sudden darkness and the hectic clamour of the birds, coming at the end of a nerve-straining day. He could not speak for the others, but they both seemed glad to have something more active to do than sit groping for pearls in the slimy bodies of shellfish.

The housekeeper stoked the fire and put the pot on. The rest of them tidied up the camp as well as they could by starlight.

While they were doing this they saw the reason for the sudden darkness. A black mass came over the western rim of the island, swallowing the stars as it advanced.

Wind and rain came down together. The wind eddied over the rim and screamed as it rushed among the trees, making them groan and crack. The rain battered furiously on the leaves and in a moment burst through in streams. The fire hissed, spluttered and died in smoke which was lost in the darkness.

Lightning exploded with thunder on its heels. The storm gods held a wild dance about the mountain, stabbing it with zigzag daggers from every side. During the vivid flashes the lagoon could be seen rising up in waterspouts to meet the rain. Some birds were swept about like sheets of paper and then vanished. Small branches flew through the air or ran along the shore.

The men crawled to the storehouse. It gave them no physical shelter after the first few minutes. But they huddled close together. They could not have heard each other if they had shouted. The thunder and its echoes, the din of wind and water, were continuous. But there was some comfort in another body, even as wet and cold as one's own.

A storm of such violence might have been expected to

pass quickly. But it continued for many hours. Almost all the time the lightning kept up its frenzied dance about the mountain. Wind and rain slightly relaxed their fury only to come again. Often and often what seemed to be the peak of the storm was the prelude to something worse. And the sky was always black.

At long last it ended, as suddenly as it had come. The wind dropped. The rain stopped. The black cloud cover split and a blue sky shone through. It was no longer night. It was a day as fresh as an English spring. But the lagoon was covered with floating leaves and many of the trees were as bare as in an English November.

4

The chart which they had made of the lagoon had been marked off in squares. Numbered posts upon the shore made it possible to identify these square areas on the water. They dredged an area, then ticked it off on the chart and moved to the next.

One day Geoffrey, Harry and Red were fishing in the western quadrant of the lagoon which was all that remained for them to work. The water was shallow, which in itself made dredging easier—so long as the bottom remained sandy. But there were patches of coral and weeds in which the dredge was inclined to catch and become damaged. Harry volunteered to fish these by diving. Geoffrey approved.

It was a scorchingly hot afternoon when every movement was an effort. Geoffrey and Red leaned over the gunwale and watched Harry swimming with a slow frog stroke over what looked like beds of many-coloured flowers and ferns. He remained below for about half a minute and then came up with an oyster in each hand. He rested with his hands on the gunwale, talking enthusiastically of the cool beauty ten feet down. Then he dived again.

So the fishing progressed pleasantly but slowly—slowly because the oysters were difficult to find. Sometimes, Harry said, he only located them by the bubble of air which rose as they snapped shut at his approach. The other two congratulated him on his skill. They were enjoying themselves too. All they had to do was to take the oysters which were handed to them, keep their heads wet to prevent sunstroke and gaze down at the gloriously coloured beds over which Harry's muscular body moved so gracefully.

Occasionally he had some difficulty in freeing an oyster when he had found it. As he explained on coming up, it is difficult to get purchase under water.

"Don't try to make it sound difficult," said Red.

Harry laughed, and duck-dived. They saw him find something and work at it with one hand, his legs beating. One foot seemed to touch a blossom of brilliant green flecked with yellow. Immediately this became a whitish mass. Harry let go of the oyster, curved his body upwards and tried to swim to the surface. But though his arms swept powerfully he did not rise.

The other two, drowsily admiring in the heat, were suddenly shocked by the imminence of tragedy. Harry, who could have scarcely more than fifteen seconds' worth of oxygen in his lungs, was trapped in some way unknown. He looked so close that Geoffrey plunged his arms and head under water, trying to reach his hands. But his fingertips were at least a yard away from them, and he almost upset the boat.

So he wasted three seconds.

Red pulled him back.

"Dredge," he said.

Geoffrey slid the dredge from the stern where it was balanced while Red with the oars spun the dinghy round and got it moving. The disturbed water hid the scene below, but pulling on the dredge rope Geoffrey felt extra weight.

"Yes," he shouted.

They heaved together. They had never experienced so heavy a load. The stern of the dinghy was forced down until water lapped aboard.

Then something gave and the rope came in. Harry's hands, gripping the dredge, broke surface. They grasped his wrists and pulled his head out of the water. His mouth opened like a balloon bursting and his eyes rolled.

When the water calmed they saw that Harry's right foot was caught in a bivalve shell as big as a gladstone bag. They knew the weight of an oyster ten inches long. A shellfish three times longer and as thick through as it was long could weigh a hundredweight or more. It was impossible to hoist it on board without danger of breaking Harry's ankle. But they managed to get him into a sitting position on the stern, legs dangling in the water.

So they rowed back to camp. Ronald waded out to meet them. They half dragged, half carried Harry to the water's edge. There with a hatchet and a hammer they slit the muscles which worked the hinge and opened the shellfish to the full extent. They examined it when Harry's wounded ankle had been attended to. It was a tridacna,

184

a giant clam. The crenellated edges of the pair of shells were made to close upon each other like interlocking fingers, or the jaws of a trap. Fully opened, the clam lay as it had lain under water. But the green and yellow mantle, the flowing fringe of the body which had camouflaged it in the lagoon was now crumpled like a wrung-out rag. The creature was a soft and shapeless mass. It was difficult to believe that it contained a complex of nerves and muscles which in its own element had made the heavy white shells spring shut at the touch of a toe.

"I promised your sister to bring you safely back," Ronald said solemnly. "But for Red and Geoffrey I'd not have kept that promise."

"She would have blamed me, not you," Harry said laughing. He was in a highly excited state. "Some men are born to trouble as the bubbles fly upwards."

Chapter Seven

I

Ronald, Harry and Geoffrey sat looking at the dark silk sheet of the lagoon. The night was absolutely still. For a long time they were silent, each thinking his own thoughts.

Then Harry said, "How will the North Star and the Great Bear look?"

"As welcome as everything else at home now that the work is done," Ronald answered.

"Home? You look on this as home."

"Not until my family is here. It takes a family to make a home."

Again they were silent.

Geoffrey looked at the tall mass upon the left which cut a slice out of the starry sky.

"I feel that I must climb that mountain before we leave," he said.

"The day we arrived I was determined to climb it immediately," Harry said musingly. "And I never have. There has been so much to do."

"Do you still want to?" Geoffrey asked.

"Not particularly. I suppose I've changed."

"You have. We all have," said Ronald. "But want to or not, we'll all be climbing the mountain now—to look out for the cutter."

"She is not due for ten days."

"That is true, and Sandy is the sort to arrive on the very day. But a ship must obey the wind, and I'm thinking it will do us no harm to keep a look-out from up there—now we have nothing else to occupy us."

"You old slave driver," Harry murmured.

"I watched for weeks and weeks before I spied the whaler," Ronald went on imperturbably. "We owe it to Sandy and Bruce and the boys to greet them as soon as they appear. They'll have had a duller time than we. So —this is Saturday. On Monday we will carry dry sticks and green fuel to the summit. From then on we will always have someone up there in daylight, to light a signal-fire as soon as they heave in view."

Again they were silent for some time. Then across the water of the lagoon came faintly the creak and splash of oars.

None of them made any comment. Although they could not see the boat they knew that Red had stopped fishing and was coming back. They knew how far off he must be and how long it would take him to arrive.

After a while Harry rose and walked towards the landing place.

When he was out of earshot Geoffrey said, "Don't you think you are asking for trouble?"

"How?" Ronald asked.

"Sending those two to the top of the mountain. They will see the whole of Skinner's territory."

"It is mostly trees," Ronald said.

"There are also open spaces. If they spotted a woman——"

"It's not likely. I know the view from there—bright

light and dark shadows. The cave is a long way off."

"But suppose one of them does see a creature walking on its hind legs. It would be such a shame to spoil everything now, at the last minute."

"Geoffrey, I'm always grateful for your advice. But I know what I'm doing. If I did not keep them busy there might well be trouble. There are ten days to fill. I can't order any more dredging. We all know there is not an oyster bigger than a penny left in the lagoon."

"Watching from the mountain in shifts will leave a lot of spare time."

"Two hours is enough at a stretch up there in the sun and wind. That means two climbs a day for each. It's quite a climb in the heat. And between-whiles we'll finish off the rafting of the shell. You'll not find there is much energy left over for exploring."

"I hope you're right," Geoffrey said doubtfully.

"I am. It's a sin to boast, but by God's grace I have done what I set out to do. There was a crisis, and a bad one, but we got over that by straight talking. I told a lie to those two, but it sits easy on my conscience, for it was proved justified. There has been no trouble. Why should it start now?"

"Those two are becoming restless and on edge."

"It is just that we are near the end and they are tired. They are good boys. I can handle them."

From the landing place came the voices of Harry and Red, greeting each other. Geoffrey was glad to change the subject.

"One of the most striking things to me about our expedition is the friendship which has grown up between those two. Their education and background could not be more different."

"But they are the same type underneath. That is a virtue of this life. You see a man for what he is."

" 'A man's a man for a' that.' "

"Aye, Robbie knew."

Geoffrey smiled in the darkness. The nearer the arrival of the *Loch Corron*, the more Scottish Ronald became. Even his accent was richer. But—most curiously and paradoxically—he had also grown a little bit like Skinner. How, it was difficult to define. But one felt it. Were they also the same underneath?

Red came bustling up.

"Has Harry been pulling my leg? You don't expect *me* to climb that thing."

"I do."

"Who's going to do the fishing, then?"

"You'll only watch by day. What have you caught tonight? Let me see. Good man! That'll make a fine breakfast."

"You can't get round me like that. Is there no rest this side the grave?"

"Not this side the cutter. But then you'll sit and think of all the things you haven't done to tell them about at Whitstable—in that public house just back of the harbour. There will be a bonus for the man who spots the cutter, just as there is for the man on a whaler who shouts, 'There she blows.' It would be something to say you had seen her mast come up above the horizon."

"You've the gift of the gab," Red grumbled. "But one day, my dear schoolmaster, I'm going to skin you—alive."

On the following Tuesday morning, Ronald, Red and Harry began going through the stores and equipment to see what was worth taking home. It was a matter which needed care and preparation, for—particularly if the cutter arrived on a day when the wind was fresh—the embarkation would have to be done quickly.

"We'll not need the dredge," Red said. "I'd like a holiday from dredges before getting back to Whitstable."

"Dismantle it and we'll stow it away," Ronald said. "It will be useful when I come back and the young oysters have grown."

"No one is going to touch it where it is, are they?"

"Best to stow it away . . . Harry!" Ronald raised his voice. "How is the food tally going?"

Harry came out of the store shelter with a piece of paper in his hand. He read out the quantities remaining—flour, rice, coffee, sugar, salt beef, biscuits and so on.

"Quite a lot as you see. They will not be likely to want any of it on the cutter. They'll be fully stocked."

"They will have been at sea quite a while before getting here. Best take it all to the cove. Then whatever they may need will be handy."

"Take it *all* to the cove?"

"Let's get it outside and divide it into loads. You'll see it's not so much."

They began doing this. It did amount to quite a lot.

"Rifles and ammunition. They will be useful here when you come back," said Harry.

"They might rust if we left them."

"Ronald! There are four rifles and nine hundred and ninety-nine rounds. Also forty-nine poor orphaned shotgun cartridges. What the devil do we want with those on the cutter?"

"Better take them. It would be a pity if they got spoiled."

"What about the dinghy?"

"I don't think Sandy will need her. But we will carry her to the cove, just in case."

"What about the pearls? Do we want them?"

Ronald looked puzzled for a moment—then laughed.

"Sorry to be troublesome. I don't like to risk keeping the cutter waiting for anything once she heaves-to."

"Talking of pearls," Red said. "I've been thinking about the monster I found. She looked dull 'cause she was dirty. All she needs is a polish. Let's have a look at her, Ron."

"Geoffrey packed them up with rice to stop them rattling. It would mean emptying the demijohn. You had better talk to Geoffrey about it."

"He's mean about it. Jealous."

"Tell him so. It is time you started up to relieve him."

"I can't go now. I've just started this job."

Red, sitting with his back against the store shelter and his legs wide apart, appeared absorbed in his task of dismantling the dredge.

Ronald did not move.

Red raised his head and their eyes met.

"What is it, Ron?"

"You are doing exactly the same thing as when I first saw you."

191

Gradually a smile spread across Red's round face.

"All right, I'll go," he said, rising.

For a fraction of a second Ronald looked puzzled. Then he smiled, and turned back to Harry who had been silently preparing loads for portage to the cove.

A few minutes later they were startled by a wild, exultant shout. Red who by that time had gone a hundred paces on his way had stopped and was pointing up at the mountain.

Ronald and Harry ran to the shore to be clear of the trees. From the summit of the mountain a feather of smoke was flying.

"It can't be the cutter," Ronald said.

"Why not? What else are we looking out for?"

"Sandy would never arrive early—eight days early. He'd not expect us to be ready."

"So all this work——" Harry began softly, and stopped.

Red came galloping back.

"He's sighted her! Won't be long now! Do we go straight to the cove?"

Harry said, "It's not the cutter. Ronald says it can't be. Geoffrey has made a mistake."

Red looked questioningly at his friend and immediately backed him up.

"Geoffrey's reliable. We all know that. But of course he don't know an East Indiaman from a Thames barge."

"If it's a whaler and she puts in at our signal, there will be some fun," said Harry.

"That's right. We can't swallow all those pearls."

Ronald stood thinking. He gave no sign of having heard the other two.

He said, "I'm going up to have a look. I'll take a rifle.

192

If it's the cutter I'll fire one shot. If it is not the cutter I'll fire three shots. Then you must stand by here and wait for me and Geoffrey."

He slung a rifle on his shoulder, put some cartridges in his pocket, and ran off.

3

More than half the circle of ocean was hidden from Ronald by the mountain as he climbed. The rest was empty. He was following the route which he knew to be the easiest and by which he had led the others on their climb the day before. After the first hundred feet it ascended on the Toe side of the buttress which swept up from the pass near the cove. Ronald might have traversed back over the buttress and thus gained a view of the rest of the circle. But that would have meant difficult and therefore slow climbing. He decided that it would be quicker to follow the easy route to the summit. He would also avoid the risk of missing Geoffrey.

When he was three hundred feet from the summit he knew that Geoffrey must be close by the clamour of birds above. One flock was already showing its disapproval of him. The men met under the onslaught of the combined flocks—thousands of diving, swerving, screeching creatures which used every means fair and foul to discourage the intruders.

"The cutter," Geoffrey shouted.

"Are you certain?"

"Of course I am. I lit the fire."

Although there were plenty of good holds and the basalt

rock was sound Geoffrey was in no mood for an argument at that time and place.

"You are quite sure it is not a lugger or some other rig?"

Geoffrey nodded.

"I am going up to see. You had better come too. Give me the telescope."

On the summit Ronald focused the glass—although he scarcely had need of it. The cutter was close enough to be unmistakable. She was racing towards the island, full before the wind, from the direction of Australia.

"She will be off the cove in less than an hour. Why didn't you signal earlier?" Ronald asked.

It was quiet at last. The birds had given them up and the only sound as the two men stood upon the table-top summit was the gentle flapping of their loose clothes in the wind.

Geoffrey hesitated to answer. When the sail must first have been visible he had been looking the other way, trying to spot people in Skinner's territory—a more interesting occupation than looking at a dazzling, empty ocean where he did not even expect to see anything.

"I lit the fire directly I was certain. I could not get it to go at first," he said.

Then he started violently, as Ronald fired his rifle.

"Why——?"

"To tell them it really is the cutter. Come on, Geoffrey. Let's get down. In fifty minutes we'll be talking to them! Less!"

Ronald's eyes were shining.

A few minutes later Geoffrey called out, "Please go slower."

Ronald paused and looked up.

"We ought to hurry. It's easy as a staircase."

"I dare say. But I hate going down. And these birds. Please keep close in front."

After that Ronald slackened speed. The mountain hid the cutter, but he still talked of it, conjecturing on what the crew had been doing during the last three months and by which way round half the world Sandy would decide to go home. Geoffrey paid little attention. He was pre-occupied with the descent, which was still a good deal too fast for his liking. And any thoughts he had to spare were for Skinner. He had not said good-bye to Skinner the day before. He had said that he hoped to visit him again during the ensuing week. But he had told him what would be the meaning of the smoke signal . . . Geoffrey wondered what Skinner was thinking. Naturally he would be relieved that the danger to his Heaven on Earth was over. But perhaps his feelings would be a little mixed. They had enjoyed their talks. They had become great friends.

Near the base of the mountain Ronald crossed over the buttress and stopped, looking at the camp site through the trees.

"I can't see them," he said.

"Harry and Red? But they would never wait in camp!"

"They should have. Now I must go straight to the cove."

"What about the kit?"

"It depends what Sandy wants to take."

Both men were breathless. Their faces shone with heat and excitement.

They ran along to the rim and plunged down the steep slope to the crack and the cove. Harry and Red were there. They had brought only their personal possessions with them. They were walking up and down the constricted space like caged animals. They shouted to the other two as they approached, asking how near the cutter was.

"Off the Heel by now," Ronald answered. "Why didn't you wait in camp?"

"You fired once. Why should we wait?" Harry asked.

"To help with the kit. But it doesn't matter."

"Nothing will matter in ten minutes," said Red. He could not keep still.

"Did you see her from the rim?" Harry asked.

"No. She will be approaching close under the cliffs, as we did. We have got ten minutes. Let's try to get these rafts into the water."

"Are we really going to take all that shell!"

"Of course we are, Harry. It's worth a lot."

"You said Sandy would be in a hurry to get off."

"He will not be in too much of a hurry for a few hundred pounds."

They worked as if their lives depended on it.

The rafts had been mounted on rollers. But the sacks of shell were extraordinarily heavy. The rollers sank in the shingle and stones jammed under the rafts. The four men paused, gasping and sweating.

"We must wait until they arrive," Ronald said.

"They should be here."

"It's only a couple of miles from the Heel. You said she was there a long time ago."

Harry and Red, who had been so lethargic packing up

in camp, were now restlessly impatient. They were half angry with Ronald because the cutter was taking longer than he had estimated.

A shining white vision floated into the narrow arc of blue visible from the cove. She was tall and brave and beautiful, and the sun-blackened, half-naked men upon her deck showed off her paces to best advantage. She swung round in a majestic curve and came up into the wind close to the cove. Her sail shivered. Arms waved. A cheer came across the water—and was sent back again.

Ronald's party, who a moment before had been snapping at each other, were now all smiles. They did not speak after that one spontaneous cheer. They waded into the sea without noticing it.

Very soon a boat put off, Johnnie and Dean were rowing, Sandy at the helm, Old Bruce and Willie remained on board. To all appearances Sandy was unconscious of anybody on the shore. He watched the water in front, moving his body slightly from side to side to get a better view. He took the boat through the broken water of the cove-mouth as if it were the easiest thing in the world.

Hands grasped the gunwale, hands were clasped. Teeth flashed in smiles. Eyes shone.

"All well, Ronald?" Sandy asked.

"All well, thank God. And you?"

"Fine, every one of us. Pearls?"

"More than I hoped. You have come early."

"We had half a gale behind us for a week and fresh winds all the way. The last three days have been the first ease-up we've had. There's no slowing the cutter now she's homeward bound. I just looked in to see how you

197

are. I'll clear off and come back on the day you name."

"We are ready now," said Harry.

"We have been ready for days," said Red.

Sandy waited for his brother to speak.

Ronald said, "I've not had time to bring the stores over from the camp. How are you off for stores?"

"Plenty of everything except biscuits. There has been little time to cook."

"We can bring biscuits. Nothing else?"

"No—except a few breakers of water, maybe. If you are ready we had best be off while the wind is fair. Back round the Horn is the way at this season, I've been told."

"There is this shell."

"It's a wee bit rough for towing rafts," Sandy said. "But you've got it in sacks I see. We could load them into the boat. We will have it all on board in three hours."

"Well, let's get started," Ronald said. "Can you spare a man from the cutter?"

"Bruce can hold her with his own hand. But we will need someone extra strong to bring the ballast up and cast it oversides and stow the shell in its place."

"Willie is the lad for that," said his brother Johnnie with an angel's smile.

The next three hours were of unremitting labour—harder than any similar period of hard work in the last three months. They all helped to load the boat with shell. Then Harry and Red transported the remaining bags to the water's edge. Meanwhile Ronald and Geoffrey went to the camp for their personal kits, the rifles and the demi-john of pearls. Back in the cove again, they found that Harry and Red had volunteered to change places with the oarsmen. So Ronald and Geoffrey with Johnnie and

Dean took a load of empty breakers to the camp—to return with the water, biscuits and ammunition. They made portage after portage over the rim while the boat party continued to ferry out the shell.

Shortly before sunset the work was finished. Ronald went out to the cutter with the final load, the demijohn held between his knees. Sandy was still at the helm. He had piloted every ferry journey with perfect skill. But this time, just as they were leaving the cove, a wave leaped on board and Geoffrey thought, 'Now Ronald's luck has broken. Now we lose everything.'

But he was wrong. They suffered no more than a soaking. Ronald smiled and shook the water from his hair. The oarsmen laughed and pulled harder. Five minutes later they were all on board the cutter with every single thing which they had decided to load.

They had worked themselves into a state of hurry and they did not pause even then. Bruce at the helm let the *Loch Corron* fall away from the wind. All sail was set, the boom run far out, and the cutter leaped forward as the wind took hold. The sun was touching the horizon.

The four men of the land party looked at the island slipping away from them. There was nothing moving on it. Not even the white tern had come to say good-bye.

Chapter Eight

I

When they were clear of the island, running swiftly but easily with the steady wind, the water hissing and sighing at the cutter's sides, the stars coming out in the velvet sky to shine in their tens of thousands, superb and calm—then the wound-up busyness of the men began to subside.

Except for Dean who was cook that day, the men sat or lay in a group about the tiller and binnacle and began to talk. Question and answer came at first spasmodically, then faster and faster until sometimes half a dozen voices were speaking together. The incidents mentioned followed no rule either chronological or of relative importance. Geoffrey made them laugh with a description of climbing the mountain under the attack of birds. It was capped by a story of how Johnnie had got into mischief with a Chinaman who sold vintage eggs. Then there was something about the coastal trading with which the cutter had earned her keep, and a technical description by Sandy of native sail-making. Remarks on the advantages and disadvantages of dredging for oysters led Harry to tell what it felt like to be caught by a shellfish—but in such a way that in their carefree mood they all treated it as a great joke. Every now and then Dean's serious, spectacled face appeared through the hatch, and he remained there listening for a few minutes while a delicious smell of food came drifting up from below. That reminded them that they had eaten nothing since breakfast, more than twelve hours before. The talk died down as they waited for the meal.

"We will get the story straight when we have eaten," said Ronald. "There is no hurry now."

"Someone," said Sandy, "will have to mind the tiller."

"Can't we lash the helm?" Harry asked.

"No! Mind you, I'm not saying she wouldn't sail true. But it's the principle with the whole crew aboard there must be someone at the helm."

Johnnie whispered something to his brother, and then said aloud, "Willie will take the helm if we bring him up some food."

They all laughed, and the good-natured Willie grinned from ear to ear.

Dean's face reappeared at the hatch.

"Supper's ready. I have done the best I could," he said in his gentle, apologetic voice.

They filed down into the cabin—and burst out laughing and praising him. He had prepared a regular feast with good things brought from the last port of call for this particular occasion. The swinging table was loaded, its centre-piece a huge, colourful bowl of apples. The eight men crowded round it and chattered with their mouths full like a children's party. The fish and meat vanished. The fruit began to disappear and the cabin grew hazy with tobacco smoke.

"Haven't you forgotten something, Dean?" said Red in a moment of silence.

"What is it you are wanting?" Dean asked, looking worried.

"We all know the skipper's rules. But on an occasion like this——" Red made the gesture of raising a cup.

"Coffee will be ready in a minute," Dean said.

"Coffee!"

Sandy said, "You shall have all you want to drink when we reach port."

"After Lord knows how many thousand miles! That's just unsociable. And it's not practical. We've a night of talk before us and my throat's dry already. Ron, ask the skipper to be human—just for once."

"What harm could there possibly be in a drink. We're no babies," Harry said.

The crew of the *Loch Corron* looked with shocked wonder at the two speakers.

Ronald glanced questioningly at his brother.

"I am sorry, boys," Sandy said. "I have never permitted drinking alcohol at sea, and I'm not going to countenance it now."

"Just a glass all round."

"Not on a ship that I command."

There was a silence.

Ronald got to his feet and worked his way to the door.

He reappeared with the demijohn.

"Rum?" said Sandy.

"This kind will do us nothing but good."

Ronald emptied the fruit bowl. He uncorked the demijohn and poured out its contents in a white stream.

They all leaned forward from their places and stared into the bowl. It was half full of rice.

The ship's party stared blankly or glanced enquiringly at Ronald like men who have failed to see a joke. The land party was stupefied. They ran their fingers through the rice. But there was nothing else.

Red broke the silence.

"It must have been one of those women."

Again there was silence, but of a different sort—the smouldering silence while a fuse is burning. Then came the explosion which blew them all on to their feet—the land party with clenched fists and burning eyes, the crew gaping, shocked but still utterly puzzled.

"You gave them the pearls," Ronald shouted. "Which of you was it, you or Harry? You unspeakable blackguards!"

"Mind what you're saying," Harry shouted back at him across the table. "Neither Red nor I gave any pearls to anyone. But I saw you pocketing some before you went out of camp one Sunday."

"I had them improved. I——"

"Improved! No doubt they looked better on a woman's bosom——"

"Hold your tongue or stick to the point. You know you are responsible. Don't you see what you have done? This is no time for lying."

"Or being self-righteous. Did you think we believed your fairy tale of searching the other half of the island and finding nothing, you and Geoffrey——"

"Good old Geoff—more in him than I'd thought," Red put in mockingly. "Going off with his butterfly net! Did you pin them out nicely and paint their portraits?"

"Since you are always so right it must have been Geoffrey. He put rice with the pearls. But the magic must have worked the wrong way."

"The rice was to stop them rattling. They were all there when I packed them up," Geoffrey said hotly.

"And I demand to know how they went," Ronald shouted. "Don't you realise everything is wasted? All those months of work. All my years before. Everything!"

"Whose fault is that? There is nothing you can do about it now. It's no use crying over spilt pearls. It's too late!"

The cutter, running joyously before the wind, gave a sudden shiver and roll, throwing the men off balance. The bowl was upset. The rice went everywhere.

"Sit down!" Sandy thundered. "Let me get to the bottom of this."

Ronald, controlling his anger but unable to keep the bitterness of frustration from his voice, told him that he had some two months previously discovered that there was a harem beyond the mountain. For the sake of peace to work in he had kept this secret—or thought he had. But the long and the short of it was that one of the women must somehow have got hold of the pearls.

Sandy nodded grimly, his eyes like nail points hammered through a block of oak.

He said, as slowly and impressively as if he were speaking from a pulpit, "It has not been easy working the ship short-handed, refitting her, earning our daily bread. We believed that you were living harder than we were, nearly as hard as the folks at Corron who have been managing without their men. Well, well. That's said and done with. Now for the future. I am not going back to my family with nothing but a disreputable tale of secret gallivanting."

"I am not going back to Corron without the pearls," Ronald answered briefly.

Sandy nodded with tightly closed lips. Then he said briskly, "That's settled then. Every man on deck!"

They hurried up the companion-way without a word.

Willie looked up pathetically from the tiller.

"You promised to bring me some food," he said.

Sandy took the tiller from him.

"Away and forage in the galley, lad," he said.

Willie went below, looking slightly bewildered, but not ill-pleased.

"Mainsheet in," Sandy ordered. "Jump to it, Harry. You are all under my orders now. Stand by to jibe!"

The boom though close-hauled came over with a violent jolt. The cutter shuddered. Blocks banged and canvas flapped while the men worked at the ropes. The waves struck them beam on. The *Loch Corron* leaned over, bowing her head into the ocean, tossing it high. Then she settled down to the long struggle back.

While they had been running with the wind there had seemed almost none. Now it buffeted them. The business of tacking—loosing ropes from cleats, drawing in other ropes, making them fast—was complicated by the darkness. They were constantly going about, zigzagging towards the island against their enemy the wind. The crew were well occupied. But only Ronald kept silent. The others had to talk, to find out, although they were for ever interrupted—by the Skipper's orders, by the

205

mate who was determined to get some discipline into the land-lubbers, and by the ship itself which threw them about.

Harry was defiant, Red his boastful echo.

"When did you find out?" Geoffrey asked.

"Before you went trotting after butterflies. I met one——"

"Where?"

"Under water."

"Ready about! . . . Lee-oh!"

Then the bull bellow of old Bruce, canvas flapping, ropes dancing, and the deck tilting the other way.

"You were cave diving?" Geoffrey asked.

Gradually, telegraphically, and with more exasperating interruptions than a serial, the story came out. Very soon after landing on the island Harry had gained the impression that there was something in the lagoon at night of which there was no sign by day. He had noticed movements in the water, phosphorescent flashes, long before the mermaid incident. But he had not risked making a fool of himself by insisting on it. He had preferred to scout out the mystery and make any discovery himself. Once he had glimpsed a creature fairly close. After that he saw nothing for nights on end until he grew discouraged in his quest.

Then, swimming into a cave, he had seen in the dim light the outline of what seemed a human form swimming along the sandy bottom beneath him. He had dived and grappled with the creature. In a flurry of panic it had turned and fought, scratching his face, holding him under until his lungs were almost bursting.

"What happened?"

"Ready about . . . Lee-oh!"

"I broke free and swam for my life out of the cave."

But his curiosity drew him back. He saw the creature again, and this time stalked it into a cavern from which there was no escape.

It was a woman—a girl. Amazingly, she spoke a little English. Her name was Etia.

"Ready about!"

Johnnie and Dean did their work, but kept as close as possible to Harry, and when they went on to the other tack again crouched close to his side, listening silently, avidly, but with an air of guilt.

There were a number of caves, Harry said. One had a great domed chamber which could only be entered from the lagoon side by swimming under water, but there was a small entrance from the landward side too. There Etia speared fish by torchlight. But for the most part their meetings had been in the water, swimming together by night. Her long black hair streamed out, sparkling with phosphorus——"

Harry checked himself with a laugh and reverted to his truculent tone.

"But I got tired of always being in my wrong element."

Ronald spoke for the first time.

"This Etia must have the pearls."

"Don't jump to conclusions."

"Unless there were others——"

"There were!"

"They worked in couples," said Red.

"When did *you* find out?"

"Harry was good enough to tell me."

Geoffrey asked how the women had managed to visit

the lagoon against Skinner's orders, and under the eyes of Silver, who generally saw that those orders were carried out.

The two men laughed.

"Silver sent them," Harry said.

"I don't believe it!" said Ronald.

"That's right," said Red. "They were the guards, sent to keep an eye on us from the southern side. Poor dears, they got so bored!"

A little before dawn the wind began to ease. Half the crew went below for a scratch breakfast. Ronald managed to speak to Harry with a certain amount of privacy.

"Have you any idea who took the pearls?"

"I have not," Harry said.

"There is no need to be aggressive. We are all in the same mess."

"We certainly are! And we will only make it worse by going ashore. What do you hope to achieve?"

"I mean to get the pearls."

"How?"

"I am asking you for help, Harry."

"If you had asked it two months ago——If you had taken Red and me into your confidence instead of lying to us——"

"I acted with the best intentions——"

"The kind the road to Hell is paved with!"

Ronald saw that Harry was desperately tired and strained. They all were, for that matter.

He said, "I need your help. If you do not know the thief, can you at least name the other women who came to the lagoon?"

"No. There were no formal introductions."

"How could they have known where the pearls were hidden?"

Harry looked at him with bloodshot eyes.

"How often did you count over your miser's hoard under the lamp? You could not see twenty yards. But did it never strike you that anybody could have seen you— let alone natives who can scout like animals?

"Why did you not warn me?"

"Because you were treating Red and me like a couple of fools. Because you never thanked anybody for advice. But I'll give you some now. Tell your brother to turn the cutter about again. Go back to Corron."

"Do you really expect me to do that?" Ronald asked.

"No, I do not. That's the devil of it."

Chapter Nine

Under the dim light of the old crescent moon a black wall rose up above the mast. At its base was a ghostly, undulating line. There was a continuous noise—a sullen murmur, hisses and sighs, winded grunts.

The cutter went about and ran away. From the crests of the swell the silhouette of the whole island was visible astern—the horizontal line of the cliff top and the tall spire. From the troughs only the mountain stood out against the paling stars.

They went about again, and the dark mass which was once more in front of them began to have depth as well as outline. They could distinguish the undercutting of the cliffs before they turned away from them on the other tack.

All this while the leaders—Sandy, Ronald and Bruce— were discussing in the cockpit. Sometimes their voices rose, and there were signs of temper in their faces. . . .

As the sun threw out its arms and glared over the horizon, the cutter was hove-to off the cove. It was almost exactly twelve hours since she had left it.

Sandy gave his orders—quietly, with complete assurance. Bruce, Willie, Harry and Red would remain on board. He himself with Ronald, Geoffrey, Dean and Johnnie were going ashore to get the pearls.

They rowed to the cove, beached the boat, climbed to the rim, traversed the shelf and walked rapidly through the forest. It gave to Geoffrey in his weary state a curious sense of unreality to be back on the island, hurrying through the dawn. He had not been told any details of method. Neither of the Mackintosh brothers said a word.

Ronald's first remark was that they were near the cave. Thereupon Sandy told Dean and Johnnie to stay where they were and await orders. They were close to the clump of sugar cane where Geoffrey had surprised one of the girls when he was chasing the bird-wing butterfly. How long ago it seemed!

Fifty yards further on Sandy stopped again.

He said to Geoffrey, "Ronald is in charge of the land party. You may take your orders from him."

Ronald said, "We are going to get back our property. I am not concerned with anything else. If Skinner behaves accordingly there need be no trouble."

"I am certain he has not got the pearls himself," Geoffrey said.

"I am keeping an open mind," said Ronald. "We'll just have a peep first of all to see who is there."

They went cautiously on. The sun was coming up above the rim. Under the trees there was a patchwork of bright light and dark shadows. The three men reached the edge of the bowl and looked into it.

Two girls were standing beside a fire above which a big pot was suspended. Others were strolling back from the lake, combing out their hair. Three came from the direction of the farm, carrying fruit and vegetables and singing as they walked. Others appeared through the curtain of creepers which hid the mouth of the cave. Last of all Skinner and Silver came out.

His people greeted him.

Then they all turned towards the East. For a period of something like a minute they worshipped in silence— standing, kneeling or prostrated according to their various religions. It was done very simply; it was strangely impressive. Immediately it was over they relaxed like any other family after morning prayers.

Ronald whispered to Geoffrey, "Do you think they are all there?"

Geoffrey counted. One man and twenty-one women. He nodded.

Ronald and Geoffrey walked down towards the group. Sandy hesitated for a moment, then caught up with them.

When the people saw them they remained at first quite still in whatever attitudes they happened to be. They seemed suddenly frozen. There was no doubt that the surprise was complete.

Skinner spread his arms behind him, much as a hen holds its wings when there is danger for its chicks. His fingers moved, urgently. If he said anything it was inaudible to the approaching men, but all the women except Silver went into the cave. The creepers swung back into place behind them.

Skinner, his arms gradually dropping to his sides, stared at the approaching men.

"You evidently did not expect us so soon," Ronald said.

Skinner blinked. His Adam's apple went up and down. He shook his head.

"Did you imagine we would go right away?"

Skinner looked at each of the faces in front of him. His

eyes were those of a man who has lost his way and is searching for landmarks. Geoffrey longed to help him but was afraid to speak. The atmosphere was too tense.

"You know why we have come back?" Ronald said.

Skinner answered in an uncertain voice.

"I am completely at a loss. I saw you go last night. Down wind. I watched you out of sight. I confess that I relaxed. Gratefully. You had kept your side of the bargain."

"Yes," said Ronald. Then very slowly, "We have come back for the pearls."

"You—you left them behind?" Skinner said blankly.

Sandy, who had maintained a grim silence, made a strange sound deep in his throat.

Geoffrey broke in quickly.

"We had them in a demijohn which was hidden near our camp. It was finally corked up two or three days ago. We took it on board without examining it. When we were at sea we found that the pearls had been removed and rice substituted for them. One of your people must have done it."

"One of my people," Skinner repeated. "How could that be? You said it was hidden near your camp."

"Yes."

"They never went anywhere near that."

"That is not true," said Ronald in a low, hard voice. "The other two members of my party have confessed that for the last two months or more they have been meeting certain of your—your people by night."

"Meeting them? Where?"

"That I do not know. But they first met in the lagoon."

Skinner's mouth dropped half open. He turned and looked at Silver who was standing behind him. Silver's

face was white with fury and her dark eyes smouldered.
She said not a word.

Skinner turned to Ronald.

"What you say is a terrible shock to me. I can only
suppose that you have good evidence. I am sure you
would never make such an accusation——"

Ronald interrupted.

"One of your people stole the pearls. We have come
back for them. I hope I make myself clear."

"Perfectly clear. Yes, perfectly clear," Skinner said.
He had regained control of his voice, but he spoke abstrac-
tedly, as if he were thinking hard. "May I ask who this
gentleman is?"

"I am Alexander Mackintosh, in command of the
cutter, *Loch Corron*," Sandy said. "My brother has told
you the position. But I must add that I cannot keep my
ship waiting."

"Quite so, Captain Mackintosh," Skinner said. He
turned back to Ronald. "From what you tell me, we have
both been deceived. Although not doubting your word
you will understand that I wish to make my own enquiries.
But in any case you may take it for granted that I am fully
responsible for anything which any of my people may have
done. You will suffer no material loss."

"What do you propose to do?" Ronald asked, stressing
the last word.

Skinner glanced over his shoulder, not this time at
Silver but at the creeper curtain of the cave.

"Shall we take a little stroll?" he said in a conventional
tone, and set off towards the lake.

The three men followed him. Silver came last, walking
stiffly and staring ahead.

214

Skinner halted. He said—in a quite different tone:

"I assure you, gentlemen, that I shall not keep you waiting on this island any longer than necessary. But I must ask you to remember that we are dealing with Orientals. Any attempt to force the pace would only defeat our common purpose. It would be best if you retired to your ship——"

"We will not get in your way," Ronald said.

Sandy broke out, "This is all very well. But if the wind rises——"

"The wind, Captain Mackintosh, is not in my control. My people are. If any of them have your pearls I shall recover them for you and enable you to leave the island with the least possible delay. You may be quite sure of that."

"How will you set about it?" Ronald asked before his brother could speak again.

"Leave it to me—and to Silver," Skinner said.

He turned and looked at Silver.

For ten seconds or more she remained silent, her lips compressed. Then she burst out in a torrent of foreign words.

"She promises that you will get justice," Skinner said.

2

Dean and Johnnie had cut themselves sticks of sugar cane. They had skinned these and were chewing them. They looked up grinning as the three men joined them.

"We will be here for a while longer," Sandy said. "You

had best get some sleep. I am going to have a look at the cutter. Where will I see her from?"

"The cliffs yonder," Ronald answered, pointing. "It's not above half a mile."

Geoffrey ate some of the food which they had brought with them. Then he lay down in the shade. He kept awake until Sandy returned and said that the cutter was lying hove-to off the cove—no trouble there. After that he dozed.

He slept fitfully. He had troubled dreams—from which he woke to hear Ronald and Sandy talking in low voices. He dropped off again—and the talk became muddled with his dreams . . . Sandy was arraigning Skinner in a court of law. He said that the prisoner had been treated much too mildly. He was an immoral ruffian, a pirate who had stolen women. He had been hiding away, for there were a score of charges against him which he had tried his utmost to evade. Ronald was speaking for the defence. He agreed that justice must be done. But it was a case of first things first. The pearls came first. In any case Skinner and his people would all be turned out when the families from Corron arrived. Ronald spread his arms like a preacher in a pulpit. "Patience and restraint," he said. "We used patience to get the pearls in the first case. We will use patience to win them back . . ." Skinner was being hanged from the crosstrees of the cutter. The women were in revolt. Harry and Red were fighting their companions. The island was on fire . . .

"There is Skinner coming," Ronald said.

The sun was high. It was almost noon. Skinner was walking slowly towards them. Sandy, Ronald and Geoffrey went to meet him, leaving the two boys asleep.

Skinner was perfectly composed. It was impossible to read anything from his face.

"You have not the pearls with you," Ronald said.

"I have discovered who took them—or, to be more precise, I have evidence which points very strongly towards the culprits."

"There are more than one?"

"Two."

"Go on," Ronald said.

"Silver persuaded me to leave the preliminary enquiries to her. She was right to do so. She is closer to the others mentally and also more fluent in the lingua franca which has developed among those who have little English——"

"Quite so," Ronald said.

"My people have what we call the Common Room— a large chamber of the cave. They have been confined there since your arrival. I have forbidden them to go to their personal retiring places which are over there." He pointed along the lake shore. "Silver has been interviewing the women one by one in her own room in the cave. A slow process, you understand. It is not just a matter of question and answer, but rather of patience, suggestion and gentle probing—playing upon personal idiosyncrasies. She is brilliant at that sort of thing. She succeeded in proving your statement that half a dozen of the younger girls—seven to be exact—have fraternised with your companions, Mr. Mackintosh."

Skinner paused, and for the first time Geoffrey saw in his face a hint of what he was suffering. He felt a pang of sympathy.

"Go on," Ronald said.

"But none of those seven took the pearls, nor any of the

others whom Silver cross-examined. She continued to question them until she was quite satisfied upon that point. So the series of interviews continued until only two girls were left."

"What had they to say?"

"Nothing. They had gone—vanished. I came immediately to give you the information."

"Did they take the pearls with them?" Ronald asked.

"Yes—unless they had already concealed them outside. How they managed to escape is remarkable. In the inner recesses of the cave there are some cracks—or vents. I have always known they must go through to the outside, for one feels the passage of air. But they are in the roof, which is under a hill. It would be a dangerous adventure, to put it mildly, to get out that way. It had never occurred to me that it might be done—that anyone might think of attempting it."

"Were they seen leaving?" Ronald asked.

"No one admits it. And yet they must not only have been seen leaving, they must have been assisted in reaching the roof."

Skinner's eyes searched the three faces in front of him—then looked beyond, at the clump of sugar cane and at the fruit trees which he had planted.

Ronald asked, "When did they escape?"

"We do not know. But Silver is now convinced that the long confessions of the seven and the drawn-out prevarications of the rest were intended to divert suspicion and give the culprits time to get away. I am afraid there can be no doubt that—with the exception of my secretary who has been taking notes for Silver throughout—all the women are united in a bond to oppose your wishes. There is no profit in discussing why. But this bond certainly exists, and it is very strong."

Skinner mopped his face. He was standing where he had stopped on meeting the others, in the full sunlight. His shadow lay like a black garment at this feet. He looked tired and drawn. No one said anything. He continued.

"The fugitives, of course, cannot escape completely. You may be tempted to call up the rest of your party and hunt for them. But you must believe that I am as anxious as you are that the pearls should be recovered quickly, so I trust you will take me seriously when I point out the objections. First, I cannot help you in a search. It is possible that some of the women are only held back by fear of the others and would assist if they could. But I am afraid that most of them would be more likely to help the fugitives than you. Second, this island is full of caves and broken ground and patches of thick vegetation, yet food of a sort is everywhere for the picking. Captain Mackintosh demurred at keeping his cutter waiting at all. Your search might take weeks. If half the party had to put off in the cutter it might take months. Which brings me to my third point, the identity of the fugitives. They are the African twins, Faith and Hope. Perhaps you noticed them when you arrived, Captain Mackintosh. They stand out from the rest."

Sandy nodded. It would be impossible to imagine a more significant nod.

"They are as mischievous as monkeys," Skinner continued. "But I can't help feeling fond of them—even now. I am sure they do not realise the harm which they have done. They are children of Nature, educated by Presbyterian missionaries. They are very devout and strict to observe what they have been taught—except about wearing clothes. But the important thing from your point of view is that they brought themselves up like wild animals in the jungle. They have the stealth and cunning of black lionesses."

"You do not think that we could find them? I know this island pretty well," Ronald said.

"May I remind you it is the pearls that you are after? If pursued the girls might scatter them in the forest or throw them in the sea. One final point. I have never known them go anywhere without their spears—which they know how to use. They were once captured by slave traders. They are not likely to allow themselves to be caught by men again."

"Are you trying to frighten us?" Sandy asked. The question came out as if for some time he had been holding his breath.

"I am pointing out the disadvantages of acting on your own," Skinner said. "I am merely being frank with you. For your peace of mind, none of us have any fire-arms."

"What do you suggest we should do?" Ronald asked.

"Leave the whole thing in my hands. Silver has played her part. The time has come for me to step in. I will manage it."

Sandy burst out, "If you can manage it, what for did you not manage it earlier?"

"We will leave it to you, Mr. Skinner," Ronald said. "Come away, Sandy. Come away. He knows what he is doing."

3

As they walked away, Geoffrey diplomatically dropped behind to adjust a shoe-lace. But it was impossible not to overhear what passed between the brothers.

"I am indebted to you, Ron, for cutting me short in public to tell me that yon man knows what he is doing. Am I to suppose that you know too?"

"I do, Sandy."

"In that case will you very kindly let me into the secret?"

"There is no secret. It's just simple common sense. Skinner wants us out of the island. He knows we will not leave without the pearls. Therefore he will get them back. He is in a much better position for doing so than we are. But, as he says, he is dealing with people who cannot be hurried. We have got to be patient. Trust my judgment, Sandy. I know the man."

Ronald's reasonable tone acted like oil upon a fire.

"Personally I would be ashamed to admit that I knew a man like that. But you are different. You always have been. You are outside the rules of ordinary decent behaviour. No, Ron, you shall not stop me this time. You shall hear me out. I have got to trust you, have I? That statement puts me in mind of incidents which you have maybe forgotten. Think back to the time when we first went to school. You were a bare-footed, snotty-nosed brat, but you happened to be better at the books than the rest of us. Therefore your parents must scrape and save and your brothers must do without so that you can go on with your learning. What happens? You go to Oxford while we labour at Corron. But before you ever win any letters after your name you decide there is an easier way to what you're after, and off you go around the world. We have got to trust your judgment. What do we get for doing so? An old coat you are said to have been drowned in—which nearly kills our mother with sorrow as our father was killed by hard work. Then up you turn again with a fine story of how we are all to live happy ever after. We are to leave the arrangements to you. We are to trust your judgment. So all Corron builds a ship for you, and you take your pick of the men, leaving their womenfolk to fend for themselves while you go off to find a fortune. You find it this time. But just a wee bit carelessly you allow it to be stolen by some hussies who happen to be hanging about your camp. That's no more than a slight inconvenience, however. We will get the pearls back if we are patient and trust your judgment. You are different from the rest of us. You have your own mysterious way of doing things."

"I have explained—" Ronald began, and was immediately interrupted.

"You have explained all right. We are to work hand in glove with a pirate, a procurer and a purchaser of slaves. There is only one thing I will do with such a man. Don't tell me he collected that harem legally. He did not. Ron, I am your skipper and your elder brother and I am giving the orders from now on, ashore and afloat. Make no mistake about that. Yon Skinner has had his chance. If he hands over the pearls before sunset, I am prepared for the sake of peace and simplicity to leave him here

222

awhile. But if he does not hand over the pearls before sunset I will take him away on the cutter as a prisoner and deliver him to justice at the first port of call. He is a British subject, I suppose, and the British Consul will know what to do with him. Now you will tell me that is not the way to get the pearls, for maybe we will never find them hunting on our own. But I tell you that I care less about pearls than a clear conscience, and the people of Corron will understand my action better than yours when we get back to our native land which we ought never to have left."

Sandy did not cease speaking until they had approached within hearing of the two boys, so Ronald had no chance to reply.

The brothers walked the last twenty yards in a smouldering silence.

Johnnie greeted them.

"Try some of this sugar cane, skipper," he said with a smile of perfect innocence.

4

Sandy told his brother that he wished to see the old camp and to inform Bruce's party that they must wait a little longer. They would take Johnnie and Dean with them in case it seemed useful to transport any more of the stores to the cove. That would be better for them than sitting around and doing nothing.

Geoffrey was left with instructions to keep an eye on the cave.

He moved to a place from where he could see into the green bowl. There was nobody about. He sat looking at the creeper-curtained entrance, thinking pleasant thoughts about the past and worried ones about the present and the immediate future until weariness and the heat of the afternoon overcame him and he fell asleep.

When he woke the afternoon was well advanced. He saw Skinner sitting under the big tree where they had first lunched together. He waved, but could not attract his attention.

Skinner was sitting with his chin sunk on his chest. He did not move at all. Geoffrey began to feel worried. He rose and walked up to him.

Skinner remained in the same position until Geoffrey's shadow touched him. Then he looked up with a start.

"Oh, it is you, Mr. Partridge," he said. "Where are the others?"

Geoffrey told him.

"I am glad of this chance of a quiet talk," Skinner said with a shy ghost of a smile.

"How have things gone?" Geoffrey asked.

"They have gone all wrong, Mr. Partridge. I was trying to puzzle out why it has happened."

"You mean you have failed?"

"I have failed in every way."

Geoffrey's heart dropped. He stood looking at Skinner and not knowing what to say.

"There is no good in being melancholy," Skinner went on. "But I would like to tell you about it in case you can give me a clue to the problem. Please sit down. You always said you enjoyed my punch. Let us have a stirrup cup."

"By all means," Geoffrey said, worried and wondering at the little man's courage.

Skinner opened his mouth as if to call, but closed it again. He got to his feet and went into the cave. He came back with a gourd and two coconut cups. He filled them. They drank. Geoffrey could think of nothing to say.

But Skinner began to talk.

"I don't *understand*. I worked everything out so carefully. I gave them all they could want—much more than they ever had before. They seemed happy. They seemed to like this island as much as I did, and to be as interested in the plans. But now——"

"They refuse to help?" Geoffrey asked.

"Absolutely. They have some justification. The last three months have been very disturbing for them. They were all perfectly contented before that. But the totally unexpected arrival of a party of men, the alarms and restrictions it caused—Then the cutter coming, and going, and coming back. And finally the scene this morning—the hostile words they must have overheard—the way I had to confine them to the cave and have them cross-examined, acting on the face of it as if I had sided with you men against them——"

"You think that is the reason?"

Skinner sadly shook his head.

"No, not really. I wish it was. But if they were as I believed them to be they had no need to be upset by the presence of men in the other half of the island. I can't persuade myself, I'm afraid, that the initiative of the meetings was all on the part of your friends. No, the fault must lie further back. It must lie in my planning, or my handling of the plan. I can get nothing out of my people now. It just seems as if they are bored. Bored and angry. I don't believe they care what happens so long as there is a change."

"You have spoken to them yourself?"

"Yes—at length. I did not merely make a sentimental appeal. I explained the situation as it is and how it could be put right by their co-operation. A child could have understood where their advantage lay. The only thing I did not tell them was of Mr. Mackintosh's intention to bring here a lot of his own people and turn us all out. I thought they might believe that the loss of the pearls would stop him. I am personally sure that with a man of his sort it would have the opposite effect—make him all the more determined and ruthless. I had hoped to arrange some compromise before you originally left. But you left so suddenly, a week before you expected. And it is impossible in the present atmosphere. But to return to my people—I might just as well have been talking to a brick wall. At last I gave up and came out here to think in peace. Silver is still trying, but only because she never gives in."

"It is a serious situation," Geoffrey said.

"Yes, it is. I don't know what can change it. I cannot put my finger on the fault."

Skinner had once more sunk into the abstracted mood in which Geoffrey had found him—the chief clerk absorbed in trying to balance the accounts.

Geoffrey said, "I overheard Sandy Mackintosh telling Ronald that if you do not produce the pearls before sunset he will take you away as a prisoner and hand you over to the law."

Skinner raised his eyes and looked at him.

"Are there charges which could be brought against you?" Geoffrey asked.

"Yes," Skinner answered quietly. "The navy were after me more than once, and the authorities of other countries too. I often had to take the law into my own hands—which means that I put myself of the wrong side of it."

"Then what shall we do?" Geoffrey asked.

"We will have another drink, Mr. Partridge. Let me refill your glass."

"But surely there is something to be done!" Geoffrey said.

"Nothing that I can think of, Mr. Partridge. I feel sure that Captain Mackintosh is a man of his word, as I know his brother to be. I cannot get the pearls. So—" He shrugged his shoulders. "If one tries something and fails one must take the consequences . . . Your health, Mr. Partridge."

"Your health, Skinner."

Geoffrey began to drink slowly and thoughtfully. He finished it at a draught and banged his mug upside-down upon the ground.

"I know what to do. Go and hide. It will be dark within an hour, and before dawn you can be safely stowed away."

Skinner stared at him wonderingly.

Geoffrey shook his arm.

"I am sure you know a good place. Of course Ronald and Sandy will hunt for you, as they will for the pearls. They'll turn the island inside out. But they will have to go in the end. At the very worst it gives you a sporting chance. I'll say you were in the cave or something. I'll try to put them off searching as long as possible."

"You would do this for me?" Skinner said softly.

"You are my friend! I would do anything for you!"

"I will never forget this," Skinner said.

But his voice had suddenly become hard. His expression had changed. His eyes which were like bullets were no longer on Geoffrey's face.

Shocked and puzzled, Geoffrey turned to follow the direction of his stare.

Sandy and the others were approaching.

5

Both Geoffrey and Skinner rose to their feet. They stood watching Sandy, Ronald and the two boys coming towards them down the slope of the green bowl. Geoffrey became conscious of another presence. Silver was standing close to Skinner.

Sandy and the others approached slowly, none of them speaking, and, when they came near, all looking intently at Skinner's face.

Ronald asked Skinner what he had to report.

"I have not been able to discover anything about the pearls or those who took them," Skinner said. "I have tried to help you. I have not succeded. There is nothing more that I can do."

He spoke quietly and with dignity.

Ronald stood looking at him angrily for some moments. Then he said:

"Skinner, you have been treated with the utmost patience and consideration. Everything you asked—time, freedom from interference—was granted you. I gave you my confidence. You tell me you have failed. But I tell you plainly that I will not leave the island without the pearls. If you will use your influence to assist in the search which we shall begin immediately we are still prepared to be generous. But if you oppose us in any way it will be very much the worse for all concerned. What have you to say to that?"

"I have very little more to say to you, Mr. Mackintosh," Skinner answered. "You say that if you are opposed it will be very much the worse for all of us. How much worse? Tell me, why do you want the pearls so badly? That you may be enabled in your own good time to bring a large number of your kith and kin and turn us all off the island. Is that not true? So what is your offer of generosity worth? I will tell you. It is a device intended to save you trouble. Do not be afraid. I will not hinder you. I could not stop you coming here and I cannot prevent you staying as long as you think worth while. But I will not try to help you any more. You have chosen your road and you shall be allowed to follow it to its appointed end. Search the island which you have appropriated. If you wish to search the cave I shall arrange to have it cleared so that nobody gets in your way. That is all I have to say to you. Do what you will."

During this bitter, quietly spoken speech, and for something like ten seconds afterwards, Geoffrey looked anxiously at the faces of the two brothers. He expected Sandy to burst out at him and have Skinner removed at once. But Sandy remained as still and silent as a cliff. And Ronald only spoke one sentence.

"We will begin with the cave."

"Wait five minutes," Silver said.

No one spoke after she had gone into the cave. To Geoffrey the sense of tension was almost intolerable. Without thinking what he was doing he moved from Skinner's side and joined the other group.

Skinner did not appear to notice this. He had not once glanced at Geoffrey.

The women filed out of the cave, Silver coming last. They moved along the foot of the cliff and stood in a group. The men watched them.

"None of them has the pearls," Skinner said coldly.

"Follow me," said Sandy, and led the way into the cave.

The creeper curtain fell into place behind them. It was dim and the air struck cold after the heat outside. At first they could see nothing except an uneven line of wavering lights. After a little while they began to distinguish the borders of the passage. They advanced slowly, following the lights. In some places long icicles of rock hung from the roof. Others rose from the floor to meet them like images in clear water. When Johnnie struck one of them it hummed like a Jew's-harp. There were also mushrooms of rock, cataracts of rock, fairy castles, things shaped like the ears and trunks of elephants, all damp, all glimmering weirdly in the light of the coconut oil lamps. From somewhere in the inner recesses came a solemn drip of water like a drum beat timing a slow march. The passage curved. It was very difficult to keep a sense of direction.

"Have you been in here before?" Ronald asked Geoffrey.

"Yes," he answered.

Sandy gave him a look. Absurd though it was, he was made to feel guilty.

"Guide us," Ronald said.

Geoffrey had only a vague memory of the cave. He found himself entering Skinner's chamber.

Sandy grimly examined it, then told Geoffrey to lead on.

So they groped their way about the cave. When they spoke their voices echoed back to them, queerly distorted. But they searched slowly and systematically. The pearls would have had to have been cunningly concealed to have escaped them.

"We will go outside," Sandy said.

It took a little time to find their way back to the entrance. As they emerged the sun sank below the rim. The long shadows melted into twilight.

Skinner was sitting under the tree, Silver standing at his side. After a minute or two the women went slowly back into the cave. None of them took any notice of the men. They did not appear to see them. To Geoffrey at least it gave an uncomfortable feeling, as if he had suddenly become invisible.

When they were some distance away Sandy said to them, "You had better all know the plans right away. We are going to have a good look for the pearls and the two black women who took them. I am not taking Skinner aboard until we're ready for him. I am going to the cutter now. Johnnie, you come with me. You others can sleep in the old camp. We will meet there an hour before sunrise."

Under the beautiful dawn sky next morning, while the birds wheeled and cried about the mountain, Ronald as the best acquainted with the island explained how the hunt was to be made. He spoke in brief sentences, clearly and with energy, as if giving orders for a military operation.

That day they would search only the western end of the island. They would stop the passes to make certain that no one could escape from the area or slip into it after it had been combed.

They began by ferrying in two loads to the southern side of the lagoon, opposite the camp. Dean went to guard the pass on that side while Willie took back the boat, on his way to the shelf which he was to block. The rest of them spread out in an open line which stretched from the rim of the island to the lagoon shore. Thus arranged they moved forward. Although they often could not see their neighbours in the line it was always possible to keep position, for they were walking across a slope, in a clockwise direction round the lagoon. Thus each man followed a contour, neither climbing nor descending. Speed was harder to regulate, for they were not permitted to call out to each other. To meet this difficulty Ronald gave himself a roving commission. He travelled continually up and down the line, telling each man if he was lagging or pressing too far forward, and assisting in the search of any particularly thick clump of vegetation or complex outcropping of rocks. He was tireless, and he kept alive in all of them the sense of urgency and the vital importance of care in what they were doing.

Birds, monkeys and other animals were swept forward by the line of men. Geoffrey was struck by the number of even small insects which he noticed. The line advanced at a pace which allowed the ground to be combed very throughly indeed. When Skinner had suggested that it

232

would take a long time to find the Africans, he had reckoned—Geoffrey thought—without taking into account the meticulous thoroughness of the Scotsmen.

It was evening before they had worked right round to the northern pass. There Willie, who had dutifully stationed himself in the middle of the shelf, told them that he had seen nobody all day. They were all tired, scratched and dusty, very hot and very thirsty, but they all felt certain that they had satisfactorily disposed of the western half of the island.

Johnnie was left on guard. Sandy took Willie to the cutter to relieve Bruce. The rest of them went to the old camp.

Then Geoffrey and Red rowed over to the other side of the lagoon, Geoffrey to take over the southern pass for the night and Red to see if there were any fish in his net or on his line which he had left set.

The watch which Geoffrey kept reminded him of what Ronald had told him about his first night on the island. The only place where he could sit with any comfort at all was the tortoise track. To either side of him were thick, thorny bushes, and beyond them the mountain face on one hand and the cliff drop on the other. The only way to guard such ground in darkness was by listening, and nothing is a greater strain upon the nerves than listening intently all night long. He was very glad indeed when Bruce relieved him in the morning.

That day they searched the other half of the island. Harry, at his own suggestion, climbed the mountain and kept watch with a telescope from the summit. The rest of them, with the exception of the guards at the passes, worked over the ground as systematically and thoroughly

233

as they could. But they had a considerably more difficult task than on the day before. The topography eastward of the mountain was more complex, the vegetation was denser in places, and the area considerably larger.

In the course of their wanderings they saw a number of the women who appeared to be going about their farm and household duties very much as usual, except that they were always in couples. They took no notice of the men. If spoken to they did not answer. Their expressions were sullen.

Geoffrey from the distance saw Skinner sitting under the tree. But Sandy was also in sight at the time. He did not try to speak to Skinner.

That evening Geoffrey was free of guard duties. He was very glad of this, for he had never felt more weary in his life. And yet somehow he could not go to bed at once. He wanted to talk to someone.

As he wandered about picking up sticks for the fire he came upon Harry who sat clasping his knees, staring out over the lagoon.

"You saw nothing from the summit?" Geoffrey said.

"Nothing that we are looking for," Harry answered. "But I saw a great deal. I saw the past and I tried to see the future. I wonder, and I wonder what this island is destined for."

Geoffrey looked down at him curiously. He had not moved. His eyes were still on the dark water of the lagoon.

"You did not want to come back," Geoffrey said.

Harry did not appear to hear him. But at last he said. "A man who says good-bye to a girl and comes back is a fool. A man who goes away without saying good-bye and comes back is—something worse."

"That is your personal reason," Geoffrey said. "But didn't you advise Ronald to go back to Corron without trying to recover the pearls?"

"Ronald is an ass," Harry said. "I felt sure he would go for the man and ignore the women—which is not wise behaviour in any country. But I know no more about the pearls than the rest of you, if that is what you are thinking about. Nor does Red."

"Do you think Ronald will get them back?"

"Yes, I suppose so," Harry answered. "One can generally get a thing when one does not count the cost."

"In that case do you think he and Sandy will leave Skinner behind?"

"No, they won't risk that—whatever moral reasons they give for their action. They are practical men. They would be afraid that Skinner might make it difficult for them to return. So it will be an island of women. Poor things. And poor Skinner. By the way, tell me about Skinner. I have not had a chance to ask since that ugly moment of truth upon the cutter."

Geoffrey told him. It was not the amusing story he had looked forward to telling. It was serious and sad. He concluded with a description of their last conversation when Skinner had let slip the opportunity to run away and hide.

"His failure seems to have broken his spirit," Geoffrey said. "And yet what most concerned him was the why and wherefore of it. He has that sort of mind. He was puzzling over just where his plan went wrong."

"I can see one bad miscalculation," Harry said.

"What's that?"

"Thinking that women who have a good reason for hating men would therefore try to avoid them. But the real trouble was the million to one chance of his dream colliding with another, here ... Come on, let's go to bed."

6

Geoffrey was wakened by voices from a deep sleep, his first for many nights. His body remained as heavy as a sandbag, but his mind worked resentfully. He felt that he had only just dropped off, and now he probably would not get to sleep again. He supposed that the cause of the disturbance was Red, who had gone fishing again, and must have just returned. Why the devil could Red never do anything without a blare of trumpets?

But the voices which he heard were those of Ronald, Sandy and Bruce. Sandy and Bruce had gone to the cutter for the night. But for some reason they had returned, and they were talking in Ronald's shelter which was quite close to Geoffrey's.

He raised his head upon his forearm and listened.

"Is the horizon clear?" Ronald asked.

"Aye, what I could see of it. But I tell you the glass had dropped three millibars since I turned in."

"Confound the glass. I know the weather here. I assure you there is nothing coming that you need worry about. Probably no more than a puff and a bit of rain."

"A wise sailor takes his barometer seriously," Bruce enunciated.

"The wind may rise. I'm not denying that. But

neither quickly nor very much. The bad storms—you can see them on the horizon and you can feel them in the air. It's heavy and full of electricity. There is no need to panic just because the glass drops."

"I am not panicking, Ron. I am only taking ordinary seamanlike precautions. It was a significant drop for so short a time."

"Are you afraid the cutter can't ride out a capful of wind?"

"With enough searoom I am afraid of nothing short of a typhoon. But off these rocks and with only one man aboard——"

"Very well then," Ronald said. "You are skipper. If you insist we will have to do as I said."

"Very well," Sandy agreed. "But I don't like it. We had better call the others right away."

Ronald came to Geoffrey's shelter and told him to get up and go to the camp fire. By the light of the flames he glanced at his watch and saw that it was half-past twelve. Harry joined them and stood with his hands in his pockets, saying nothing.

"Are the others on guard?" Sandy asked.

"Dean and Johnnie are."

"It's the land party I want to talk to. Where's Red?"

"Fishing. He told me he might be late because he would have to mend the net."

"I can hear him now," Harry said.

They all listened. A faint sound of oars came over the lagoon.

"I'll tell him later," Sandy said. He turned to Geoffrey and Harry. "I came ashore because I found that during

237

the last few hours the glass has dropped considerably. My brother assures me from his local knowledge that that portends nothing serious. I am sure I hope he is right. Nonetheless, as skipper of the cutter I do not feel justified in endangering her by keeping her hove-to off this coast. Therefore she must be sailed out of danger before the wind makes it impossible to row out to her. That is a plain rule of seamanship. You can't take risks in a typhoon area. But the difficulty is this. My brother feels strongly opposed to leaving the island at all at this moment. He believes, and I am bound to respect his view, that if we are absent even for a day or two the situation may change to our disfavour. To put it bluntly, we may not get back the pearls. Well then, we have been forced to arrive at a compromise—which is this. A party will go at once to the cave, apprehend the man Skinner and take him on board. So he will be out of the way. The ship's party will then sail the cutter clear of the island. If we only have a small blow we will be back as soon as it is over. But should the weather turn really bad—I am being perfectly frank with you—I might decide it was best to run to the most convenient port and hand Skinner over to the law before returning. In that case we might be away some weeks—which would give you of the land party plenty of time to recover the pearls. That's how things are. Any questions?"

"Yes," said Harry. "Is this Ronald's plan?"

"The main points of it."

"Ronald," said Harry, "at least one member of the land party is not prepared to stay."

"Please don't make silly objections," Ronald said lightly. "As you have just been told, it may only be for a

238

day. You can judge the weather as well as I can and that's what I think."

"We saw how long it took to beat back after only two or three hours, and without a storm. Good intentions will not alter that. I know the thin end of a wedge when I see one. I'm in a hurry to get home."

"So are we all. And the sooner we get the pearls the sooner we can go home."

"Ronald, if the cutter sails, I sail with her."

"What are you afraid of—that she won't return?"

"Not specifically."

"Of the women then? Skinner won't be here. Are you afraid of women? What could they do?"

"That, Ronald, is a question which every man since Adam has asked at one time or another. Nobody has ever guessed right."

When Ronald next spoke his tone had hardened.

"You must admit that I have never used my weight as leader. But when you volunteered to come here you put yourself under my orders. I order you to stay."

"I suppose I can be forced to stay," Harry said. "But I would be a mutinous element, worse than no use to you."

"Go if you wish," Ronald said angrily. "We can do without him, Geoffrey, can't we?"

Geoffrey said nothing. He did not like the plan at all, yet did not like to back Harry against his leader.

"I'll force no one against his will," Ronald burst out. "But I am staying—if need be, alone. I have done it before and I'll do it again."

"Don't you see what you would be doing then?" Harry said. "You would be putting yourself in the place of

Skinner—with the difference that every one of the women was at your throat. I know for certain that one of those twenty swam out to Skinner's ship because she had killed a man."

"Red is hailing us," Bruce said into his skipper's ear.

The boat was close enough for them to see the phosphorescent bow wave rising and subsiding at each stroke. She was being rowed with energy. Every now and then Red made a breathless attempt to shout. They were all glad of this change of interest.

Red stepped overboard into the shallow water. He pulled the bow up on to the shore, then hurried to the fire.

"Listen, the position is this—" Ronald began.

Red interrupted him.

"You don't know what the position is. You can't. I've found the pearls."

"You have what?"

Red, all eyes upon him, stood in the flame light, panting. He got back his breath.

"I've not got them with me but I've got someone who knows exactly where they are and will take us there. My girl——"

"Your—" Sandy broke in.

"My girl. I'm trying to tell you. We ought to start as soon as we can, so I got to give you the main points quick." Red, though still short of breath, was talking as fast as a street salesman. "She came running from the trees when I was over there mending the net. She didn't steal the pearls. She didn't think she'd manage it. She's not that sort. But she told those two blackies to do it. Why? Because she wanted to stop me from going. Well, we sailed. That made her cry! She went to bed in the cave, with the pearls under her pillows. She never spoke to a soul. She could trust the blackies who are her special pals. But when we turned up again she knew the cave would be searched so she told the blackies to take the pearls and scramble out and hide till she came to them in a special place where they'd once met or something. The other women don't know the place. But one of them that helped the blackies up to the roof of the cave discovered what was in their leather bag. So they all knew, for they're thick as thieves—all except Silver that is. They wouldn't tell Silver, or Skinner. Not on their lives. They don't want Skinner to hand them back to us and let us go. I daresay they want them themselves. Or they want to work off old scores on us, and him. I didn't have time to find out even if Young Bamboo knows——"

"Young Bamboo!" Geoffrey exclaimed.

"That's my girl's name. I'm only telling you enough for you to see it's genuine and act quick because that's our only chance, and hers. The women don't trust anyone, even each other. That's why they've been going about in pairs. But Young Bamboo is trusted by Skinner and Silver, so she stayed with them a while and managed to slip away from the others. But she thinks she was followed, which I don't doubt because the silly little thing has on a white dressing-gown you could see in the dark at half a mile. She risked her skin to get in touch with me."

"How did she get over the pass?" Sandy asked.

"Easy enough. She knows a shelf up on the mountain where you can't be seen from below."

"Where are the pearls?" Ronald said.

"Far end of the island somewhere."

"That's vague enough!"

"I knew you'd be suspicious so I gave her the promise she wanted and tried to fetch them. But we couldn't get through. Those women are roaming all over the place. We'd have got caught. Then—well, you wouldn't have got the pearls. So after trying for an hour or so we turned back. Johnnie didn't even see us coming back. I rowed her over."

"She is here?"

"In the boat. She's shy. She'll come out when I tell her it's all right. But we'll have to be careful or she might be seen against the fire. We don't want those wild cats sprinting round and stopping the pass. That's why I said we'd have to start soon as possible."

"Steady a minute," said Sandy. "Whoever is giving the orders, it's not you."

"I'm only *telling* you," Red wailed.

"You are telling us to go rushing off through the night behind some wild woman who as likely as not will lead us into a trap."

"I suppose you can wait till tomorrow. But I don't advise it."

"Red, boy. I am not waiting till tomorrow. I am taking the cutter off tonight because there's a big drop in the glass."

"Fifty thousand pounds worth of pearls and you are afraid of a drop in the glass. That's what comes of being a teetotaller." Red waved his arms. "All right, leave them behind. They're not mine. I'll be glad to go. But we'll have to take Young Bamboo. I promised her that— swore by my God was how she put it—when she swore to guide us to the pearls. Besides, she will be murdered if we leave her. They'll all know what she has done—broken

242

their bond or whatever you call it. And she did it for us."

"I will not have one of those women on my ship," Sandy said.

"She's quite different—" Red began. But Ronald stopped him.

"Let us see this woman," he said. He, Red and Sandy went to the boat. Geoffrey followed them.

They saw a small figure in a kimono curled up in the bottom, half hidden by the net. A doll's face looked up at them.

Ronald asked her a number of questions. She answered mainly in monosyllables. She was evidently very frightened. But everything corroborated Red's account.

Geoffrey asked her, "When Skinner appealed to you, why did you not tell him?"

"He would not have let me go," she answered.

"Don't you see, she wants to get away," Red said. "It doesn't cost us much to take her—not in exchange for the pearls."

"I'll stand no tricks," said Ronald.

The girl looked at him.

"You don't get pearls. You leave me behind. Women kill me."

They moved away from the boat, leaving Red with Young Bamboo.

"I don't like it," Sandy muttered as he walked away. "It makes sense, I'm not denying. But I don't like it at all."

It was on the tip of Geoffrey's tongue to tell him what Young Bamboo had been. That would have put a violent stop to the plan. But he did not know who would gain and who would suffer as a result. He kept silent.

A short distance from the fire, Ronald stopped and faced his brother.

He said, "What has happened tonight proves one thing at least. The women can come and go through the southern pass as they like. So all our searching has been useless. But we have been given a chance—a thin one and a wild one if you like. Shall we take it? We could get to the Toe and back within five hours at most, so we are safe enough as far as the weather is concerned. I am perfectly certain of that. I have no reason to believe that this chance will yield anything useful. But you, Sandy, will remember the night that I came back to Corron. I told you of how I first saw this island from the *Swan*. I had no reason to believe that the interior was any less barren than the cliffs I saw. Yet I risked my life to see it. Why? Because I knew that I would never rest with the doubt in my mind that I had missed the chance of a lifetime. For that same reason I mean to try out this chance. We risk no more than a long walk."

"You've had your way since birth," said Sandy. "All right, we'll go. But I am still in command. And we go armed." He raised his voice. "Do you hear that, all of you? We are calling in the guards and going armed."

"Would you shoot women?" Harry asked.

"Not if they behave like women," Sandy said.

7

Half the party went to the cutter for weapons, the rest—with Young Bamboo—directly to the northern pass.

Geoffrey was in the party which went to the cutter. They each took two rifles and got back into the rowing boat.

Only Willie smiled when they pushed off. He settled down with one arm over the lashed tiller while the cutter, her jib a-back, nosed gently into the wind, moving no more than a grazing horse in a pasture. There was little sign of bad weather. The glass was still falling, but more slowly.

The men at the pass reported one alarm. They had heard something in the bushes. But on going to investigate they had found nothing.

They set off. The Japanese girl moved at a sort of trot, a comparatively rapid and untiring pace. Geoffrey remembered Skinner telling him that her one recreation was to go for long walks by herself. But glancing at her he thought how frail she looked—like a figure of porcelain. She never spoke. She had only a pale blur for a face. There was always someone to either side of her, and behind. Geoffrey remembered the description of the procession at Yoshiwara, and how only when she had fallen and hurt herself had the mask-like face become alive.

The way she had chosen would put the freshwater lake between them and the cave and avoid most of the open spaces. If their objective was the Toe this would add considerably to the distance. But Red whispered that this was the safest route. Young Bamboo answered no questions.

They frequently heard noises among the trees and bushes through which they passed. Almost certainly these were made by animals. But the men's nerves were kept on edge. Young Bamboo trotted imperturbably on.

245

The crescent moon rose. She floated blindly on her back through the reefs of stars. She was too old to give any appreciable light. In fact it soon became darker. A black cloud was coming up from the west. The men of the land party knew it for what it was, and Ronald persuaded his brother to go on.

Then the rain came—drenching, blinding, even choking in its force. With heads bowed and hands shielding their faces they pressed on, but very slowly. The enormous drops were beating on the leaves like a million drumsticks, and pouring through to splash in the puddles they soon made.

Young Bamboo walked on unheeding. Her kimono was sticking to her body. Her face ran with water, but it was still a mask.

The rain lasted for an hour, then stopped like a tap turned off. For some time longer there was a drip-drip-dripping from the trees, but the sky was once more clear and glittering with stars.

They were within little more than a mile of the Toe when the stars began to pale. The sky pulled on the shot-silk mantle of dawn. The birds began to twitter, scold and sing. The Japanese girl quickened her pace.

The light grew rapidly. They reached the limit of the trees, which stopped where the ground became barren. At this end of the island the rim was not clearly defined. The steepest part had been broken away by undercutting or by earthquake. The remaining ground sloped upwards gently to a slipper point. The scant bushes were bent and contorted. Weathering had sculptured the rocks into extraordinary forms. The surface was pot-holed like pumice stone, though on a much larger scale. The sun,

246

although it must have risen clear of the ocean, was still hidden by the point of land.

Young Bamboo signed to the men to fall back. She pressed on fifty yards ahead of them, picking her way delicately and swiftly over the rough ground. There was only another quarter of a mile to go. But she seemed absolutely sure of herself. She never paused. A thin mist rose from her wet clothes as she hurried on. The men followed, forgetting in their excitement to look back over their shoulders, looking only at her, waiting for her to find what they were looking for or at least to give them some sign . . . So the seconds drew themselves out and out, crowded with thoughts, hopes, anxieties—Whatever happened before they reached the tip of the island, or even if nothing happened, their future would be decided one way or another. They had not searched this area the day before. They had stopped at dusk at the limit of the trees, deciding that nobody would hide in that open, barren place. But just for that reason it was perhaps the best hiding-place of any on the island. Some of the potholes were big enough to conceal a person. There were enough to hold an ambush. What a place for a trap, this narrow point where sheer cliffs met. But the girl was still pressing on and they had to follow her. They were committed. They could not see if she was looking into the holes as she went by. The sun had risen above the cliff and was blinding them.

On the extreme point of the island Young Bamboo stopped. She stood silhouetted against the rising sun, an enigmatic Oriental figure. One arm was extended. She was pointing at the sea which was just coming into view. What did that mean? Had the two Africans——

And then they saw it—something white upon the water. Shutting out the dazzle with their fingers they stared at it. Quite soon they were certain that it was the cutter. She was scudding away with the rising wind. They could make out two figures in the stern.

Sandy focussed his telescope, and at last said, "A man and a woman. Skinner and Silver, I'll swear it. Damn them, but it seems they can handle her!"

While they stood staring, Willie joined them. He had run along the rim, keeping the cutter in sight. He panted out his story. In the blinding deluge of the storm he had answered a hail—leaned over the side to grasp the ship's boat as she came alongside—been pulled into her heels over head. Untangling himself he saw a woman with a shotgun on the cutter's deck, a strange man loosing the helm. They went with the wind.

The eight men scarcely heeded. Nothing made any difference now. They had been stranded . . . They stared after the cutter racing joyously with the wind.

They watched until she vanished over the horizon. Only then did they turn away, feeling utterly helpless and all of a sudden desperately tired.

In the shadow of the trees twenty women were waiting for them.

Young Bamboo placed a leather bag in Ronald's hands.

"You got what was promised," she said, her face expressionless.